Diary of a 6th Grade NINJA

Terror at the Talent Show

Diary of a 6th Grade NINJA

BOOK 5

Terror at the Talent Show

MARCUS EMERSON

ILLUSTRATED BY **DAVID LEE**

ALLEN&UNWIN
SYDNEY·MELBOURNE·AUCKLAND·LONDON

First published by Allen & Unwin in 2017

Allen & Unwin
83 Alexander Street
Crows Nest NSW 2065
Australia
Phone: (61 2) 8425 0100
Email: info@allenandunwin.com
Web: www.allenandunwin.com

A Cataloguing-in-Publication entry is available
from the National Library of Australia
www.trove.nla.gov.au

ISBN 978 1 76029 559 2

Cover design by Marcus Emerson and Sandra Nobes
Text design by Sandra Nobes
Cover and internal illustrations by David Lee
Set in 14 pt Adobe Garamond by Sandra Nobes
Printed in Australia by McPherson's Printing Group

1 3 5 7 9 10 8 6 4 2

www.marcusemerson.com

This one's for Elijah…

My name is Chase Cooper, and I'm a sixth grader at Buchanan School. That's a photo of me up there studying for a big test – wait, no. That's a penguin. My photo is on the next page.

If you're reading this then you probably know who I am, but for those of you who don't, allow me to give you the super-jacked, turbo version.

My favourite foods are cheese pizza, cheese toasties, and nachos with extra cheese.

I love watching awful horror movies from the '90s, corny action movies from the '80s, and the absolute worst science-fiction movies from the '70s. And I mean the worst of the worst – spaceships on strings and alien costumes where you can see the zipper.

1

ME ~~PLAYING VIDEO GAMES~~ STUDYING

CHASE COOPER

What else do I do? Well, I spend most of my free time playing video games and reading comics, y'know, typical sixth grader things. Sometimes I'll throw a book or two into the mix, just to make things interesting. It's a personal goal of mine to read at least fifty books this year. Why? Why not? Smart is the new cool.

I also like riding my bike through trails in the woods, swimming, climbing things, eating biscuits and orange soft drink, tormenting my little sister, and leading a ninja clan to defend my school against evil…

Oh, right. There's also *that*.

I'm a ninja.

I was the new kid at the beginning of y
and was recruited by a secret ninja clan that
I met during gym class. My first baby ninja
steps were pretty wobbly, but I think I handled
myself alright. After saving the day by
uncovering a shady plot to frame my cousin for
theft, the ninja clan thought it'd be a good idea
if I became their new leader.

(NINJA DOVES
ADDED FOR
EFFECT)
(Because they're
super cool)

I've been struggling to be a good leader, and I'm the first to admit that I've failed more than a few times. But life lessons were dished out and I learned a lot, which hopefully makes me a more experienced leader now. I don't know. I'm still just doing my best to make it to the end of the year without a broken face.

It's only been two weeks since Jovial Noise tried messing up the science fair. Her real name is Olivia Jones, but she calls herself Jovial Noise – I think it has something to do with being a villain or something. She left notes in my locker every day, challenging me to play along in her sinister game. In the end, good won out over evil, and the science fair was saved.

Normally, Buchanan School gives me month-long breaks between disasters, but I had a feeling that was starting to change. I couldn't put my finger on it, but something was off the second I shut the door to my dad's car.

My dad had dropped me off by the side doors of the school a little earlier than normal.

4

I needed to get to my locker and pay a visit to Zoe before seeing her in homeroom because I had to ... well, to be honest, I wanted to apologise to her.

Let me explain – the school talent show was coming up on Friday, and she was put in charge of it. Yep, the *entire* thing. Buchanan wasn't even going to have a talent show until Zoe begged Principal Davis for one. He said the only way he would even consider it would be if one of the students took charge and planned it on their own. Obviously Zoe jumped at the chance to do it. I'm pretty sure she knew how much work she'd have to put in, but she's the kind of kid that likes that sort of work. The coolest part about the whole thing is that Principal Davis moved some funding around and has offered a thousand-dollar grand prize for the winner.

On Saturday, she called and asked me to help. *'Hey, Chase. Wanna come help set up the cafeteria for the talent show? We're meeting at noon. Faaaaaaaith will be there.'*

'Yeah?' I held my phone between my ear and shoulder so both my hands would be free to keep playing my video game.

'Yep! Gavin'll be there too. You can call Brayden if you want.'

I sighed. It sounded alright until she said Gavin *was going to be there. That's just how I wanted to spend my Saturday - sitting around at school watching Zoe and Gavin giggle at each other. Sick.*

'Sorry, Zoe,' I said. 'I totally would, but did you say noon? Yeeeeeah, that's actually right in the middle of my nap, so I'm gonna have to say no. Maybe next time.'

Zoe paused. 'But the stage needs some work and Gavin said it'd be easy to set up with a few extra kids there. Can't you skip your nap to help?'

'Nope,' I said flatly.

'But you're like *eleven* years old,' Zoe said. 'Didn't you stop taking naps in kindergarten?'

'You know *I* gotta take advantage of Saturday naps while I can!'

'...serious?' Zoe asked, shocked.

'*Mmhmm,*' I hummed. *The line clicked as she hung up on me.*

I've felt guilty ever since.

After my nap, I texted her but she never replied. I thought I'd get a chance to say sorry at Sunday brunch but she skipped to keep setting up for the talent show. And that's the reason I was early to school on a Monday morning.

🛡 🛡 🛡

I opened the side doors to the school and stepped into the hallway. It was pretty early, and homeroom wasn't for another fifteen minutes. I wanted to get to my locker before going to the cafeteria to talk to Zoe, but I'm not a morning person so I was really dragging.

As soon as the doors shut, I felt a chill dance down my spine, as if Buchanan School was teasing at the fact that I was going to face some serious trials this week. I knew the actual fifteenth president of the United States of America *wasn't* a ghost out to get me, but I still balled my fist and hissed, '*James Buchanan!*'

Shaking the chills off my back, I shuffled across the carpet, feeling the weight of my drowsiness settling in on my eyelids. Man, no matter how hard I tried, I just couldn't get my blood pumping! I was tired, but not just a little tired. Like, *tired* tired.

Like, the kind of tired where my head bobs up and down until my whole body jerks awake and then I realise everyone in maths is staring at me, wondering how an eleven-year-old kid could possibly produce the amount of drool that was pooled on my desk and … never mind. Let's just say I felt like a zombie.

As I approached my locker, I clenched my jaw and gulped. Every time I opened it, my heart raced at the thought of finding another sticky note with a chess piece. Olivia's notes had stopped after she got busted, but I still couldn't help but worry.

Spinning the combination into the lock, I pulled up on the handle and flipped the door wide open, flinching as if a clown on a spring was going to jump at me.

But it was all clear. I smiled, finally able to breathe again as I stared at the pile of rubbish that was collecting in my locker. There wasn't anything out of the ordinary about any of it, except for the few spots of mould that looked like they had started growing hair and teeth.

I stuffed my textbooks into my book bag and zipped it up. As I slung the strap over my shoulder, I heard some commotion down the hall. It was hard to make out what they were saying from where I was standing, but one sentence came through crystal clear.

'That penguin got out of its cage!'

Penguin? Shutting my locker, I leaned back, making that 'huh?' face of total confusion. You know the one – you've probably made it when you've smelled something nasty but couldn't figure out what it was. Yeah, *that* face.

I followed the other students as they ran to the tinted glass walls of the cafeteria. The sound of excited shouts bounced down the hallway, growing louder as I walked closer.

'Look at them chase after the penguin!'

The penguin! I had no idea what was happening, but a sudden rush of excitement poured over me, completely shocking my body out of its drowsy state.

I made my way through the swarm of kids in the school lobby. Another chill ran down my spine, but I wasn't sure whether to be worried or not because only half of the kids around me looked frightened; the other half were laughing.

As I approached the cafeteria doors, I saw a line of boys and girls with their faces pressed against the glass, trying their best to see what was going on.

I glanced at the clock. In my gut, I *knew* it was way early, and I *knew* that Zoe would be in the cafeteria setting up for the talent show, but part of me hoped that maybe more time had passed and she would be out of the cafeteria already, safe from the ruckus. No such luck.

I pressed my face against the door of the lunchroom and squinted to see through the thin pane of glass while students beside chatted excitedly with each other.

'What happened to the penguin? Does anybody see the penguin anymore?'

'I think it went under the stage!'

'Who's Zoe chasing after? Is that dude gliding on the floor? It looks like he's flying!'

And then there was a loud crash from inside the cafeteria. Everyone in the lobby gasped.

'Watch out! He's coming at the door!' a girl right next to me shouted.

I tried to dive out of the way, but it was too late. The cafeteria doors burst open and I was knocked clear across the lobby. Rolling across the floor, I felt the carpet burn my elbows until I finally stopped against the wall.

'Outta my way!' shouted a voice.

I glanced up just in time to see a boy skid along the carpet on a scooter. He was wearing a white hockey mask so no one could see his face.

'Chase!' shouted a familiar voice by the cafeteria doors.

I jumped to my feet, baffled by what was happening. Gavin was running out of the cafeteria with two folded-up scooters, one in

each hand. Other students down the hallway
were screaming at the boy in the hockey mask.
Because of the crowded corridor, he hadn't got
far.

Gavin chucked one of the folded scooters
at my feet, and then flipped open the locked
hinge on his scooter, shooting the wheels out
from under it.

'There's no time to explain!' he shouted.
'Come on!'

I kicked at the end of my scooter, popping
the whole thing off the ground. I grabbed the

handlebar with my right hand and hopped into air, using my foot to open the locked hinge. The scooter twisted open like a set of nunchaku and snapped into shape as I nailed the landing on the carpet of the lobby. I laughed so hard that I snorted, amazed by my crazy good luck. 'Ha!' I barked, looking around. *'Did anyone else see that?'*

All the students in the lobby were too watching Gavin chase after the boy in the hockey mask. Not a single one of them was looking in my direction.

'Seriously?' I said, grinding my teeth. 'One of the sickest stunts I've ever done in front of dozens of people, and *nobody* saw it!'

Kicking the carpet, I shot forward, weaving through the crowd of students. Gavin was about six metres ahead of me, and I could see the boy in the hockey mask just a little bit in front of him.

As kids dove out of the way, I kept kicking at the floor, making my sweet ride roll faster. Finally, I caught up to Gavin.

'What's the deal?' I yelled, gripping my handlebars tighter.

Gavin kept his eyes on the kid in the hockey mask. 'That doofus set a penguin loose in the cafeteria!'

'What's a penguin even doing in school?' I asked, leaning to my left and barely missing a girl. She spun in a circle, dropping a few of her textbooks as I passed her.

'Watch it!' she shouted, annoyed.

'Sorry!' I hollered.

Gavin stomped his foot harder on the carpet, getting his scooter up to epic speeds. 'The penguin was part of some kid's talent show performance or something! Zoe had all the acts show up early today so we could test out the stage and make sure it was solid!'

'Someone's got a penguin in the talent show?' I asked.

'I guess it dances with them or something,' Gavin replied. 'Whoever this kid is we're chasin' after is the one that popped open the cage and set it free!'

Staring ahead of us, I saw that the kid had turned down another hallway. 'Why would he do that?'

As Gavin neared the corner, he jumped off his scooter and started sprinting after the masked kid. Once a couple of students were out of the way, he rolled the scooter on the floor and hopped back on at full speed. I'm not gonna lie – it was awesome.

I followed his lead and tried to the do the exact same thing, except my moves weren't as slick. Instead, I took the corner too fast and bounced off the lockers like a ragdoll.

I regained my balance and jumped back on my scooter, hoping no one saw my goof. It took a few good kicks to catch up with Gavin again.

The new hallway wasn't carpeted, so our rubber wheels picked up even more speed. Our scooters glided like they didn't have wheels at all.

The kid in the hockey mask was still far ahead of us. He must've had some pretty strong legs because he had no problem maintaining the gap between us.

'Right after everyone freaked out that the penguin was loose, one of the corners on the stage collapsed. Luckily the thing's only half a metre off the floor or it could've done some damage,' said Gavin.

'You think this kid had something to do with the stage?' I asked, kicking the polished floor beneath my shoe.

'Definitely!' Gavin said confidently. 'Once that penguin got loose, the stage collapsed, and as soon as the stage collapsed, that kid grabbed a scooter and bolted out the door.'

'Where'd these scooters come fr—' I started

to ask, but a hand grabbed at the collar of my shirt, yanking me off my scooter. It didn't hurt, but it stopped me in my tracks. I looked up and saw Principal Davis looking rather disappointed at me. Mrs Olsen, the science teacher, was standing in front of Gavin, blocking his path with her hands on her hips.

'These scooters are from the drama department,' Principal Davis grunted.

I looked down the hall but there was no sign of the kid in the hockey mask. 'He's getting away!' I shouted. 'We almost had him!'

Principal Davis furrowed his brow. 'Catching him isn't your job. You *do* understand that, right?'

I sighed, staring at the floor and nodding.

Gavin fell silent and stared at the same spot on the floor.

The principal folded his arms and chewed his lip. 'Look, I get it. I know you just want to help Zoe, but this is better left to the adults, alright? You could've hurt someone tearing through the hallways on these things, you know that?'

'Yes, sir,' Gavin and I both whispered at the same time.

Mrs Olsen huffed as she pressed her lips together, but she didn't say anything.

'Why don't the two of you head back to the cafeteria,' Principal Davis said. 'Mrs Olsen and I will handle things from here.'

'Yes, sir,' Gavin and I whispered again, shuffling our feet.

'You will both be excused from class this morning. I'll have a hall monitor let your homeroom teachers know you two are helping with the talent show.'

'One of *Wyatt's* hall monitors?' Gavin sneered.

Principal Davis nodded.

I swallowed hard, feeling a lump travel all the way down my throat, but I didn't say anything. It wasn't the time or place to mention my feud with Wyatt, the leader of the red ninja clan.

After I became the leader of Wyatt's old ninja clan, he was quick to create another one of his own. My ninjas are honourable and strive to do the right thing, but his ninjas are another story.

They exist to wreak havoc and create chaos wherever they are. Gavin and I were instructed to leave our scooters behind. Principal Davis said he'd personally return them to the drama club, but I'm pretty sure it was because he didn't trust that Gavin and I wouldn't ride them in the halls again. I don't blame him for thinking that, though, because we totally would've.

'I can't believe that kid got away,' Gavin mumbled. 'That's the sorta thing that really grinds my gears, y'know?'

'Yeah,' I sighed. 'And I'm not sure that Principal Davis is gonna be able to catch him.'

'What he'll likely do is assign the case to the hall monitors,' Gavin said. 'Which normally woulda been a good idea, but ever since Wyatt took over, I'm not sure how much help they are anymore.'

'They're all red ninjas,' I said. 'Remember the red wristbands?'

Once Wyatt took Gavin's place as the hall monitor captain, things went downhill. Wyatt has replaced *every* normal hall monitor with a member of the red ninja clan. Yep, red ninjas walk the halls of Buchanan right out in the open and in their normal street clothes. They can tell who's in their clan by the red wristbands they all wear. I haven't been able to prove anything yet, but I just *know* Wyatt is planning something big. He's *gotta* be!

And Sebastian, the school president, *has* to be in on it. He's the one who fired Gavin and promoted Wyatt, but nobody has any idea why! Sebastian was known for being a shady kid and so was Wyatt, so the two of them working together equals some sort of mega ultra supervillain duo, bent on school domination!

Gavin nodded. 'Yeah, I remember those wristbands. You don't suppose Wyatt was the kid we were just chasin' after, do ya?'

'On the scooter?' I asked, suddenly floored that I hadn't even considered that yet. 'It makes perfect sense, doesn't it? He stole my book bag a couple of months ago and took off down the hallway just like the kid in the hockey mask!'

'That kid had some moves too.'

'Wyatt? Or Hockey Mask?' I asked, smiling smugly at the nickname I'd thought up.

'Both,' Gavin said, turning down the hallway that led back to the cafeteria.

'Great!' I said. 'Then all we have to do is prove Wyatt was in the cafeteria before the penguin was set free, and then question where he was *after* all that jazz. We should be able to connect enough dots for Principal Davis to bust him once and for all!'

Gavin nodded.

The bell rang overhead. The school day had officially started. Gavin and I started jogging to the cafeteria. Principal Davis said it was cool for us to skip homeroom, and anytime I'm told to skip a class by the principal, you better believe I'm gonna do it.

**Monday.
The cafeteria.**

Gavin made it to the cafeteria doors first and held them open for me. As I stepped through, I saw the stage extension Zoe was trying to get built. It was a platform that stuck out about three metres, but one of the corners was leaning on the ground. That must've been where it was sabotaged.

On the polished floor were skid lines from the scooter that Hockey Mask had used to escape. I followed the lines all the way back to a long bench against the far wall.

Lining the bench were students who I assumed

had acts in the talent show. It must've been where they waited for their turn. The bench was under huge metal scaffolding, the kind that painters stand on to reach high places. The wooden board and paint cans on top were tipped to the side. Luckily none of the paint had spilled – that would have been a disaster.

Against the wall, I saw Zoe sitting on the floor and hugging her knees. Her face was red from crying. Her hands were balled into little fists, pinching the ends of her sleeves that she used to wipe her tears away. Faith and some other girls were by her side, comforting her.

Across the room, I saw the metal cage that must've had the penguin in it. The student that owned the penguin was sitting in her chair and staring at the cage in disbelief. I recognised her immediately. Her name was Sophia, and she was one of Buchanan's star cello players. She dressed super trendy, like she was straight out of a teeny-bopper magazine for young hipsters.

'How's a kid own a penguin anyway?' I asked Gavin.

Gavin shrugged. 'I dunno, but probably the same way some folks own monkeys.'

I shook my head, smirking. 'Man, that'd be cool, huh? A *monkey*. I'd totally train it in the art of ninjutsu. Can you imagine that? A tiny monkey ninja sidekick that drops in at the first sign of trouble?'

Gavin stared at me for a second. 'That's the dumbest thing I've ever heard.'

I pursed my lips, slightly embarrassed.

Zoe's voice cut through the air like a katana. 'This is *your* fault!'

I spun around, surprised and scared by her sudden outburst. 'Mine?'

My cousin jumped up from the floor and stormed toward me with her finger pointing directly at my face. 'If you had been here over the weekend to help, then *none* of this would've happened!'

'What?' I cried defensively.

Zoe whipped her hand out and pointed at the stage. 'The only reason why the stage isn't finished yet is because we didn't have enough people to help! If you were here, it would've been finished, and none of this would've happened.'

Gavin set his foot up on a chair and leaned against his knee like a cowboy. 'She's got a point. The only reason why the corner buckled the way it did was 'cause it wasn't latched into place – none of the corners are. I needed an extra pair of hands to do it so it had to wait until this week.'

I stared at the stage, shocked. I didn't know what to say. 'I'm here now. Can't we fix it?'

Gavin leaned over and studied the collapsed portion of the stage. 'Nope,' he said flatly. 'We're gonna have to order a new part for it. This one's busted up now.'

Zoe turned back toward me and jabbed at my chest with her finger. 'Which means the stage is going to remain incomplete for the entire week! And you know what *that* means...'

I stared into my cousin's fiery eyes. She's kind of a perfectionist. She's the kind of kid who finishes her homework *weeks* before it's due,

25

who makes a hundred lists for any sort of
activity she's involved in, who prints out a
schedule for family trips, who finishes every
single task she's given, on time and flawlessly…
you get the idea.

An unfinished piece of her talent show puzzle
was going to have her pulling her hair out all
week. It was very possible that she was going to
look like an old bald man by Friday.

'I'm sorry,' I whispered, and then I
remembered the conversation Gavin and I had
in the hall about Wyatt. 'But Gavin and I think

we know who freed the penguin and broke the stage!'

'Oh really?' said a high-pitched voice from behind me. 'And just who do you think the guilty student is?'

I slowly turned around but already knew who it was – Wyatt, leader of the red ninja clan and captain of the hall monitors.

'Wyatt,' I said, clenching my jaw.

'Sup, yo?' Wyatt replied with a mouthful of bubblegum, nodding his chin at me.

'I don't know how you got back here so fast,' I said, 'but I *know* it was you who broke the stage.'

Wyatt pushed the huge wad of pink gum into the side of his cheek making it look like he had a golf ball in his mouth. 'I've been in here the entire time!' he laughed loudly.

Zoe folded her arms. 'He's telling the truth,' she said. 'He's been at one of the tables in the corner with his cousin, Carlyle. They're one of the acts in the show.'

'Har!' Carlyle shouted as he ran forward.

Carlyle was a problem during my second month at Buchanan. He acts, dresses, and talks like a pirate in every annoying way possible. His plan was to change the school mascot to the Buccaneers, which would have officially made Buchanan a pirate-themed school. Thankfully, I stopped him.

'Seems like your facts be a little off, eh matey?' Carlyle sneered, squinting an eye at me.

I ground my teeth, super annoyed by the way he spoke. 'Seems like,' I said.

WYATT
(ninja)

CARLYLE
(Pirate)

Gavin's face twisted. I could tell he was upset that our assumption of Wyatt being guilty was wrong.

Carlyle stepped forward and put his hand on Wyatt's shoulder. 'I'll do ye one better, mate. My cousin and I even tried to *catch* that sea-snarfin' penguin when it escaped.'

'It's true,' Faith said, standing by Zoe's side. 'Wyatt was actually the first one to jump after it.'

'Really,' Gavin said sombrely. 'That don't sound like somethin' you'd do.'

Wyatt tilted his head slightly and smiled. 'Don't know if you heard yet, but I'm the hall monitor captain now. I've got a reputation to uphold.'

I watched the muscles in Gavin's jaw twitch, but he remained silent. Wyatt had just dealt a low blow to my friend.

Zoe finally spoke, cutting through the awkward silence. 'Whatever, alright? What's done is done. The only thing we can do now is clean up and try to fix things before Friday. The good news is that we have a week to sort it out.'

Wyatt and Carlyle laughed and walk out of the cafeteria. As hall monitor captain, it probably wasn't too difficult for Wyatt to skip class without a pass.

Zoe, Faith and their friends went back to the stage. They were in the middle of painting oversized banners. Zoe had chosen a bright orange colour to use for all the talent show posters. She was good at artsy stuff like that.

Sophia, the kid who owned the penguin, was talking to Principal Davis, probably giving him a detailed report of when the animal was last seen and which direction it ran away in. Just what the school needed – a loose penguin poopin' all over the place.

'So we were wrong,' Gavin said as he approached me.

'Yup,' I said. I hated to admit it, but it was the truth.

'Principal Davis said he'd handle it, and I'm inclined to believe everything he says being that he's the *principal* and all,' Gavin said.

It took all my concentration to understand

what Gavin was saying since he talked like a cowboy. 'Right,' I replied.

'But that don't mean we can't *help* the case,' Gavin said. 'Wyatt might not have done it, but somebody did.'

'Obviously,' I said. 'We weren't chasing after a ghost or ... *were we*?' I snapped my head to the side, half expecting to see the ghost of James Buchanan laughing at me from the corner of the cafeteria.

'I say we team up and try to figure this thing out on our own,' Gavin said, moving his finger back and forth between us. 'But Zoe ain't gonna be happy 'bout that.'

'Why would she care what you did?' I asked, but already knew the answer before I finished speaking.

Gavin paused for a second. 'Because we're goin' out now.'

Urgh. I wasn't sure why I felt uncomfortable, but there wasn't anything I could do about it. Maybe it was because she was my cousin and I felt like I had to protect her. Although she really doesn't need my protection. Plus, Gavin is a good guy – it's not like she was going out with *Wyatt*.

I faked a smile and nodded. Then I quickly changed the subject. 'I'm not sure what we can do to help find Hockey Mask.'

'We can ask around,' Gavin said, taking a breath. 'We'll look for clues and talk to any kids who might've seen something.'

'Okay,' I said. 'Where do we start?'

Gavin looked at the empty penguin cage across the room. 'Seein' as it's Sophia's penguin, I think we should ask her first.'

I turned my head, looking for the girl in trendy clothing, but she wasn't in the room anymore. 'Great,' I said. 'Where'd she go?'

Gavin raised his eyebrows. 'She's probably in the principal's office now. I'm sure her parents are already on their way here. We'll have to catch her at lunch.'

'That'll be good,' I said. 'Maybe she'll have her penguin back by then. Meet me in the lobby before lunch?'

'Yep.' Gavin nodded as he walked away. 'See ya then.'

I tightened my grip on my book bag straps and walked out of the cafeteria. First period would start soon, but I had a few minutes of alone time before the bell went off. I spent it on a bench in the lobby, staring at the dark red carpet where I was knocked over.

I felt awful about letting Zoe down. If I had come and helped over the weekend, this whole thing might've been avoided. *That* was the real reason I wanted to find Hockey Mask – not because I wanted to bust him, but because I felt like I owed it to Zoe. She worked harder than anyone I knew, and she totally didn't deserve this. She's nice to everyone, even if they're jerks to her.

It was easy for me to brush the dirt off and get back on my feet when the bad guys – the pirates, the red ninjas, Jovial Noise – were after me, but this time was different. This time they were going after my family.

Monday.
Gym class.

For the first time in my life, I was looking
forward to gym. The morning was still a
whirlwind of events bouncing around my
noggin, so I thought getting some fresh air
while walking the track might help clear my
mind. Good thing Mr Cooper, the gym teacher,
lets us do pretty much whatever we wanted.

I was really hoping to see Zoe in first period,
but she was allowed to skip and keep working
on talent show stuff. Maybe it was a good thing
I didn't see her though – I wanted to say
something about how Gavin and I were going

34

to scope things out on our own, but it might have actually made her angrier.

I leaned against the wall, watching students walk out of the locker rooms. Could the kid in the hockey mask be one of them? Was he watching me right now, laughing at the fact that he got away?

'Hey, man,' a boy's voice said.

I shook my head, coming back to reality. My best friend, Brayden, was standing next to me.

An interesting bit of information about Brayden – he's a self-proclaimed werewolf hunter, but he's never found a werewolf. Trust me when I say it's not because he hasn't tried. His basement is filled with maps with red drawing-pins pressed into places where there have been reports of werewolf sighting. Newspaper clippings and photocopies of books are taped to the walls like wallpaper. If anyone was going to find one of those monsters someday, it was going to be him.

'Braaaaaaayden,' I sang, jokingly. 'Whassup?'

Brayden's face twitched. I could tell he was uncomfortable.

'Something wrong?' I asked.

'I dunno, dude,' Brayden said. 'Somethin' about a penguin running loose in the school has me a little freaked out.'

I laughed and put my hands behind me, using them as a cushion against the wall. 'I bet they find that thing by the end of the day.'

'But what if they don't?' Brayden whispered with fear in his eyes.

I paused, a little surprised that Brayden, the werewolf hunter, was afraid of a tiny little penguin. 'Are you messing with me?'

Brayden gulped, and then snapped his attention to a spot across the room, the way a dog does when it sees a rabbit. After a moment, he said, 'Penguins freak me out. That's all. It's not weird.'

'It is weird,' I said, smirking. 'Penguins are just birds that can't fly.'

'I know, man,' Brayden said. 'But that's the thing that freaks me out – what bird *can't* fly?'

'Fat birds?' I joked.

'They're up to something…' Brayden said, his voice trailing off. 'Those things are smarter than you think.'

'Definitely,' I said. 'Every penguin on Earth is conspiring to take over the world by tricking us into thinking that they can't fly. One day we'll look up and see that the sky has been painted black by the bodies of flying penguins, declaring war on humans. And we'll all cry, *'Help! Please, save us!'* But the Earth will whisper, *'No.'*'

One of the girls standing nearby stared at me, her jaw wide. 'That's so dark,' she whispered.

'*Ninja* dark,' I said.

'Ninja *dork*,' Brayden said, laughing.

The bell rang at last, and the rest of my classmates stood in a line against the wall.

'Hey, Chase!' a boy to my left said.

It was Jake, followed by his friends. Jake was one of the popular kids on the football team. You know the type – tall, good-looking, perfectly tousled hair, the star quarterback with the cheerleader girlfriend. A few of his jock

SOME DUDE

JAKE

SOME OTHER DUDE

moose

moose

se

friends trailed behind him as if they were wolves following their leader. A lot of kids referred to them as the wolf pack.

'Hi, Jake,' I said.

Brayden wrinkled his nose, but didn't say anything.

'Should I call you 'moose-man'?' Jake asked. His wolf pack laughed, throwing light punches at each other's shoulders. 'Way to mess up the school's mascot.'

Let me explain real quick – remember when I said I was able to stop the school from becoming the Buchanan Buccaneers? Well, because of that, I was allowed to choose the new school mascot. But being me, I gave it *way* too much thought and chose a moose to represent the school. Of course now I see it was a huge mistake, but at the time, I was so excited!

'What's done is done,' I said in a monotone voice, trying to mask my fear. 'If I could go back and do it again, I'd pick something cooler.'

'But you can't go back,' Jake said. 'Can you?'

I shook my head. 'No.'

'Leave it to a nerd to choose something so lame,' Jake said. 'No, actually you're not even a *nerd*. You're *less than* a nerd. You're a *nerdling*, hoping to pull yourself out of the nerd-nest to spread your nerd-wings and fly to nerd-topia!'

My jaw dropped, in awe of how poetic Jake was. I tried to think of a witty comeback, but I was always bad at it when put on the spot, plus I didn't really like being a jerk. So I said, 'Yeah?

Well your mum called and uh … she said you'd make a very fine gentleman one day.'

Jake gawked at me.

Brayden leaned close and whispered, 'Dude, that wasn't really a burn. That was more of a *heal*.'

'*I know!*' I whispered back.

'Like, if this were a video game, you'd have just handed Jake a health pack,' Brayden added.

I rolled my eyes.

Mr Cooper stepped out of the locker room with his clipboard in hand. He scanned the gymnasium full of students and scratched their names off the attendance list.

Jake and his wolf pack backed away from me once Mr Cooper started walking toward the centre of the gym.

'Listen up, everyone,' the coach yelled loudly. 'We'll be doing things a little differently this week.'

I pushed off the wall and stood up straight. What was he talking about? Different? Change? No! Change is bad! Change is my third greatest fear, right under bees, and clowns on their lunch break! What? Have *you* ever seen a clown casually eating a chicken wing? Yeah, I didn't think so.

'Principal Davis is insisting on a *little* bit of actual sports activity in gym class,' the coach said. 'So this week, you'll *all* be playing football.'

My stomach sunk. The only thing I understood from football was that pressing B on the controller made my quarterback chuck the ball at the nearest available teammate!

The coach pointed at Jake and made a motion telling Jake to stand next to him. Pointing at Brayden, he made the same motion. Brayden glanced at me as he walked out to the centre of the gym.

'These two are your team captains,' Coach Cooper said. 'After the teams are chosen, meet on the field outside.'

Normally, I would've been a little worried about getting picked last, but with Brayden as one of the captains, I wasn't concerned.

41

I breathed a sigh of relief and rested against the wall again.

'Tim,' Jake said, pointing to one of the boys in his wolf pack.

Here we go. Brayden's going to point at me and—

'Claire,' Brayden said quickly.

I had already taken a step, so I had to stop myself. It was obvious enough to be embarrassing. A few students around me chuckled to themselves. Even Claire giggled as she took her place behind Brayden.

I smiled tightly. It was cool. Brayden knew what he was doing. I'd get picked second or third, right? That's *gotta* be what he had planned...right?

Jake pointed at another boy from his wolf pack. 'Zach.'

Instantly, Brayden said, 'Doug.'

Just so you know, Doug is *not* my name. What was Brayden doing? After every kid he chose that *wasn't* me, he stared at the ground. And it went on like this for the next *twenty* kids that were chosen! Suddenly, I was one of the three remaining students left against the wall. What gives?

Jake scratched at his chin, and then pointed at the short kid next to me. 'Him,' Jake said. How awful. Jake didn't even know the kid's name. I didn't either, but we'll just ignore that.

Brayden made eye contact with me, but immediately looked away. 'Charlie,' he said softly.

'*Really?*' I shouted, my voice echoing across the gym. I cupped my hand over my mouth, feeling stupid. Shaking my head, I started walking toward Jake's team.

'What do you think you're doing?' Jake asked. 'Teams are even. Get lost.'

I froze. I could feel everyone in the gym stare at me. You know what's bad? Getting chosen last for a team. You know what's worse? *Not getting chosen at all.*

The other students filed out the gym doors, making their way to the football field outside. I stood in the same spot, staring at the floor, hoping that a meteor would crash through the ceiling and vaporise me.

'Chase?' Coach Cooper asked as he stepped out of his office. 'Why aren't you on the field?'

'I'm not on a team,' I replied, trying not to sound devastated. 'It's cool though. I can just hang out in here.'

The coach shook his head. 'Nuh-uh,' he hummed. He pointed his thumb over his shoulder toward his office. 'You can't stay in here alone. We just got the mascot costume today and it's sitting on my desk. Go put it on and join us out by the field. If you can't play, you can at least run around in that thing.'

I wasn't too excited by the idea of wearing a costume, which was ironic because I was wearing my ninja costume under my street clothes at that exact moment. 'Really, it's okay if I just—'

'C'mon, son,' the coach said as he walked toward the exit.

I shuddered. I hated when anyone other than my parents called me son. Walking to Coach

Cooper's office, I saw the costume that he was talking about. It was just an oversized mask, gloves, and boots, all covered with brown fur. It looked *hideous*. Who in the world chose *that* to be the mascot? Oh right ... me.

Defeated, I put on the costume.

Five minutes later, I was out on the field wearing the ridiculous moose costume. I felt like I was working at an amusement park. All I needed was a fairy floss cart and a bunch of balloons tied to my wrist.

I stood on the sidelines as everyone else in class played football. Every now and then I waved my hands and did a happy dance because Coach Cooper suggested I do *that* instead of standing completely still. He said that 'a moose with a human body that's staring at a bunch of people is the stuff of nightmares'.

Through the eyeholes in the mask, I watched as Brayden's team did their best to compete against Jake's team. I had no idea why Brayden didn't choose me first or even at all. My ears felt warm as I grew angrier under the moose mask.

GROSS, RIGHT?

Suddenly I saw a bunch of kids running straight for me. I stumbled backward, afraid for my life. When I looked up, I could see a football spinning out of control through the air.

'Nooo!' I shouted, putting my hands up. The football missed me, but a bunch of kids on Jake's team slammed into me, knocking me to the ground. The moose mask acted like a helmet, preventing my skull from bouncing against the field.

'Sorry, man,' said the kid that tackled me. I recognised him as one of the guys from the wolf pack. He held his hand out to help me up.

And then I saw it – a red band dangling from the kid's wrist. *This kid is a red ninja!* I didn't want to seem suspicious, so I grabbed his hand and allowed him to help me up.

As I looked at, I noticed that the other two members of the wolf pack were wearing red wristbands as well. Wyatt's ninja clan reached further than I thought.

'C'mon already!' shouted Jake as he jogged over. He put his hands on his knees and caught his breath. It gave me a clear view of the red band he had around his wrist too. Jake was a red ninja.

I stared at Jake through my moose mask.

'Hey, mascot,' Jake said, straightening his posture. 'You see that Chase kid anywhere out here?'

Hesitant, I shook my head.

'He must've stayed inside to cry,' Jake said, looking over his shoulder at the gymnasium.

I shrugged, biting my lip so I wouldn't explode with rage.

Jake snickered and brought his attention back to me. 'I'd suspect *you* were Chase, but there's no way you're a dude.'

'Yeah,' one of Jake's friends said. 'You move too gracefully while you cheer.'

I frowned, upset and flattered at the same time. I gave them a double thumbs-up and nodded.

''kay,' Jake said as he picked up the football. 'If you see Chase, you let us know alright, sweetheart?'

I continued to nod, gritting my teeth the entire time.

Jake and his wolf pack went back to the football game. Apparently they were all red ninjas now, which meant they knew who Wyatt was, which also meant they probably knew I was the leader of my own ninja clan. Things were getting worse. *Much worse.*

Monday.
Lunch.

Once gym was over, I changed out of the
moose costume as quickly as I could and ran
out of the locker room. I had no desire to be
confronted by Jake and his wolf pack.

After bolting out into the hallway, I took
a hard left turn and sprinted down the hall.
Posters of Sophia's missing penguin adorned the
brick walls of every corridor.

I was supposed to meet Gavin back in the
cafeteria, but I wanted to check on my ninja
clan before their training.

The ninja clan I lead used to meet in a secret

hideout in the woods during gym class, but because of a series of disastrous events, the hideout was demolished to make room for a new set of bleachers. Since then, we've been meeting in an empty classroom near the back of the school during lunch.

I pretended to start a club called Martian Language Arts. Principal Davis thought it was a cool idea since he's really into sci-fi shows about time-travelling doctors or something, so he said I could have the room.

Saying it was to study alien languages pretty much secured the fact that no one would ever try to join it, except for the principal that one time. I had to convince him that it would've been weird for the other students if he sat in on the class. He took off his oversized scarf and walked away, disappointed. I felt awful about it, but secrecy is the most important thing to a ninja clan.

I opened the door that had the Martian Language Arts sign taped to it and stepped into the room. When I first started at Buchanan, there were nearly fifty members in the ninja clan, but over the last few months, that number's dropped dramatically. I scanned the area and only counted twenty ninjas. I wasn't sure why kids were quitting, but I haven't had a chance to look into it.

'Sir!' shouted one of my more dedicated ninjas, Naomi. She stood in front of the other ninjas, holding her mask. She whipped her short brown hair out of her face and smirked at me. 'Good to see you.'

The other ninjas in the room stood at attention and thumped their chests once, shouting, 'Ha!'

I sighed, shutting the door behind me. 'Ninjas, we've got a problem,' I said.

'The missing penguin?' Naomi asked.

I nodded. 'Seems like the penguin isn't even the real problem. My buddy thinks the penguin was just a distraction so the real crime could be committed.'

'What was the *real* crime?'

'Someone tried busting the stage,' I replied,

glancing at the clock on the wall. Gavin would probably be waiting outside the cafeteria for me. 'I've gotta run, but if you could keep an eye on the talent show set-up for anything fishy, I'd appreciate it. I know Zoe would too.'

'But what about training?' one of the ninjas at the back of the classroom said.

'Naomi can take over for the week,' I said.

Naomi smiled at me, punched her open palm and nodded once. The ninjas behind her did the same.

I walked out of the room feeling a little guilty that I had to spend another training session away from my ninja clan, but I had to shake the feeling off. There was a criminal on the loose, and I had to stop him.

Monday.
Lunch.

The lunch line was long, so I decided to skip it and head straight into the cafeteria. I knew my stomach was going to hate me for it later, which meant it would probably grumble during the quietest moment in class. I hate when that happens because it guarantees someone will turn around, point at me, and yell, 'He farted!' at the top of their lungs.

Gavin was waiting for me just inside the cafeteria. He was standing next to one of the rubbish bins, fiddling with a small notepad and scanning the room for anything that might lead us to the kid in the hockey mask.

Along the far wall was the stage with the collapsed corner. Half-painted banners were drying on it.

Eyeballing the room, I noticed it felt a little emptier than normal. Normally the lunchroom is packed, with hardly a place to sit, but at the moment it felt like half the students were missing.

'Zoe probably still hates me, huh?' I asked, joining Gavin.

He nodded, flipping open his notepad. On the first page, he had scribbled a few notes. At the bottom of the page was a crudely drawn penguin with 'Sophia' written after it.

'According to your notes, the penguin's name is Sophia,' I joked.

Gavin ignored my joke. 'Since Sophia's an orchestra nerd, she'll probably be sitting with a bunch of her orchestra friends.'

'What's *that* supposed to mean?' I asked, offended and still a little upset by Jake calling me a *nerdling*. 'Oh, so because she loves orchestra, she's automatically a nerd?'

'Calm down,' Gavin said. 'I don't mean it like that.'

'How *else* can you mean it?'

'When I say 'nerd', I mean someone who's really into something, y'know?' Gavin said. 'Sophia loves orchestra and is really good at playing cello, which means she probably practises it on her own time. So she's an orchestra nerd. Some kids like sports, right? They play, watch and talk about sports 24/7, which makes them a sports nerd. I'm using nerd in a good way here.'

Pushing my hands into my front pockets, I sunk my head into my shoulders. 'Yeah, I guess I know what you mean. Still doesn't feel right calling someone a nerd though.'

Gavin put his hands up as he continued across the cafeteria. 'Sorry, alright? I should've used a different term.'

'Fine,' I said. 'Apology accepted.'

On both sides of the aisle, students were

burying their faces in their lunches. It was pickled meatloaf day, which for some strange reason, kids at Buchanan went *nuts* over.

As we searched the cafeteria for Sophia, I overhead a few students gossiping.

'*Did you hear they still haven't found that penguin?*'

'*I heard it was a whole team of penguins that got away!*'

'*Did you know if you feed a penguin after midnight, it'll transform into a little green monster?*'

'*I think you're thinking of a movie.*'

'*Nope, pretty sure it's real life. Saw a documentary on it.*'

'*Yeah, that was a movie.*'

'*We'll see who's laughing after midnight.*'

Finally, Gavin stopped. 'There she is,' he said.

I followed as he stepped up to the table where Sophia sat. Other orchestra students sat with her, looking rather bored. She was wearing thick-rimmed glasses without the lenses in them, along with headphones that weren't hooked up to

SOPHIA

anything. Everyone at the table was dressed like they were straight out of a 1930s movie about the future, which is the standard style for hipsters.

Hipsters have a way of making others feel like they're outdated. If anything seems fresh and new, a hipster will always make a remark about how it's lame and boring already, as if they're ahead of the curve. Hipsters make me sick, almost as much as pirates, because you can never *like* anything if a hipster is around.

She glanced at us as she jabbed at her pickled meatloaf. The last part of her conversation was clear as we approached.

'…so yeah,' Sophia said to her friends. 'That new bow is about three hundred bucks, and I'm totally gonna buy it next week.' She stopped as soon as she noticed us. 'Sup?' she asked all cool.

Gavin raised his foot and set it on an empty

chair. 'Funny business this morning with that penguin, ain't it?'

'*Isn't* it,' Sophia said, correcting Gavin's grammar. 'And *no*, it's not funny at all. My penguin is still running around somewhere in this school.'

'They haven't found it yet?' I asked.

'No,' Sophia replied, her lip quivering. 'It breaks my heart to think that Hotcakes is scared and alone right now.'

I paused, choking back a chuckle. 'Your penguin's name ... is *Hotcakes?*'

'So?' Sophia snipped, annoyed.

'Is it 'cause he likes pancakes or something?' Gavin asked.

'Are you serious?' Sophia replied. 'Penguins can't eat pancakes. It's just a cute name.'

Gavin put his hands up, surrendering. 'Sorry,' he said. 'If you don't mind, Chase and I would like to ask you a couple of questions about this morning and ... Hotcakes.'

I choked back another chuckle, putting my fist up to my mouth and coughing. 'Excuse me,' I said.

Sophia glanced at her friends and sighed. They sighed in response, which was a typical hipster thing to do. It was almost like they were telling each other they were bored without actually using words.

'Fine, go ahead,' Sophia said, waving her hand at Gavin.

Gavin flipped open his notepad and clicked his pen. 'Can you tell us what happened this morning?'

Sophia's eyebrows raised as she took a deep breath. 'I got to school early 'cause Zoe said all the acts needed to rehearse. I think she was extra excited about the fact that I had a penguin in my act.'

'Who wouldn't be?' I muttered.

Sophia continued. 'So I set Hotcake's cage down by the bench against the wall. I walked away from him for like, a *second*, and then I heard everyone screaming.' Sophia's voice cracked as she covered her face.

'It's alright,' Gavin said softly. 'Take your time.'

'I'm just so worried about him,' Sophia sniffled. 'He was supposed to be back by now!'

'Yeah, we thought the school would've caught him by now too,' Gavin said.

Sophia paused, making a long face while she carefully wiped the tears away from under her eyes.

'Did you see who opened the cage?' I asked.

Through her sobbing, she mumbled something hard to understand. 'I don't know, I just…it just…Eli said…I mean, I think I saw…I dunno, okay? It all happened so *fast*!'

Gavin scribbled 'Eli' onto his notepad. 'Eli?'

Sophia took another deep breath. 'Yeah, I mean, no. I meant to say *Calvin*. I'm pretty sure I saw Calvin messing around with Hotcakes before everything happened.'

'Calvin,' Gavin repeated, adding the name to his notes.

Sophia suddenly frowned as she leaned her head over. 'Can we be done, please? I don't want to talk about this anymore. I just want to find Hotcakes and make sure he's safe.'

Nodding, Gavin said, 'Thank you for your time, and if you hear anything, please let us know.'

'What are you, like, the Buchanan detective team or something?' she asked.

I couldn't help imagining what our logo would look like if Gavin and I *did* form a detective team.

Gavin laughed. 'Nah, we just want to help Zoe get this talent show back on track, and also make sure that Hotcakes doesn't get hurt.'

'Thank you,' Sophia said, smiling through the tears running down her cheeks.

Gavin nodded, flipped his notepad shut, and started walking down the aisle. I followed him, glancing at the corners of the cafeteria. Hotcakes had been set free just that morning, so he couldn't have gone far. I wasn't sure how many exits there were to the cafeteria, but I doubted there were many.

'At least we got a name,' Gavin said.

'Calvin,' I said. 'Do you know him?'

'Surprisingly, I don't,' Gavin said. 'I thought I knew everyone here.'

'Could he be a new student?' I asked.

Gavin raised his eyebrows. 'Possibly, but I'd have heard about a new kid.'

'Maybe he's *really* new?'

Gavin stopped at the cafeteria doors. 'Maybe. We'll have to ask around some more. Sophia also mentioned Eli. He's someone I *do* know.'

'But she *meant* to say Calvin,' I said.

'I say we start with the first name she gave us,' Gavin said. 'It won't hurt our investigation, and maybe he'll know who this Calvin kid is.'

I couldn't argue with him. 'So where's Eli?'

Gavin sighed as he glanced at the clock. 'We'll have to wait until tomorrow to ask him anything. That's okay though. It'll give us time to collect our thoughts.' Gavin clutched his hands on his stomach. 'Plus I'm *starving*.'

I smiled at the thought of food. We spent the rest of lunch eating nasty pickled meatloaf and arguing who would win in a battle between cowboys and ninjas.

Tuesday.
The cafeteria.

My dad brought me to school early again so
I could help Zoe. She didn't ask for my help,
but I figured that showing up was better than
not. The few times I called her phone the night
before, I could tell she hit the ignore button
because it rang once and sent me directly to
her voicemail.

As I walked through the halls, I saw
photocopies of the missing penguin hanging
from the brick walls. 'Have you seen me?' was
printed in bold font underneath the picture.

Finally, I arrived at the cafeteria. Through the

tinted windows, I watched as silhouettes of students moved back and forth within the room, setting up more random stuff for the talent show. I pushed the doors open and stepped inside.

I'd missed out on helping the day before, so I never got a chance to see everyone working together. I have to admit – the sight was incredible.

Several kids were on the far side of the room finishing up the banners that would be hung later in the day. They were huge – at least three metres wide and one metre tall.

Gavin and some other guys were fixing up the broken section of the stage. He was shouting orders at the guys on the other end of the platform, telling them to lift their side higher so he could slip some books under his corner.

All over the room, students working on tasks Zoe had assigned them. Some were playing with the coloured spotlights, switching them on and off with the controls at the back of the room. A few kids were testing the sounding-board on it. Everyone else was in a whirlwind of activity, running back and forth, setting up props for specific acts.

On the other side of the room was the long bench where students waited for their turn to perform. It was against the far wall that led backstage. Just above the bench was the metal scaffolding with paint cans still sitting on top of it.

Zoe was a couple of metres away from me She was wearing a yellow construction hat, holding a clipboard and shouting orders into a walkie-talkie.

'We've only got four days until the show,' Zoe barked. 'And you're only telling me *now* that we've got a problem with the pyrotechnics?'

Pyrotechnics? Like, fireworks and stuff? Man, Zoe was cool. She was planning the most epic talent show in history!

'Zoe?' I said as I walked up to her.

Zoe turned around, but didn't smile. 'Chase,' she said, and then returned her attention to the walkie-talkie. 'I don't care *how* you figure it out, just *figure* it out! No more excuses!'

'Who're you talking to?' I asked.

Zoe pressed her lips together and rolled her eyes. 'Principal Davis.'

'No way!' I said. 'You didn't just *command* the principal to do something, did you?'

She set her walkie-talkie on a table nearby. 'One of our acts has a pyrotechnic display, nothing huge, just some loud pops and sparklers, but we can't test anything until the inspector comes in and says we can. But the inspector is out of town for the week, so the principal has to figure out another way to get our pyro approved.'

I gotta hand it to Zoe – if she wanted something done, she figured out how to get it done. I shuffled my feet, a bit embarrassed. 'Look, I'm sorry about last weekend. I should've been here to help.'

Zoe looked at me. 'Go on...'

'But I'm here now,' I continued. 'And I'm willing to do whatever I can to make things right, even if it means picking up a hammer and getting my hands dirty.'

'Don't you live by some ninja code or something?' Zoe asked. 'Wouldn't it have been the honourable thing for you to help family if they asked?'

'Yes, you're right,' I said, 'which is why I should've helped you.'

Zoe folded her arms. 'It shouldn't take a ninja code for you to understand how to be there for someone else...especially if that someone else is family.'

I tilted my head back, tired of getting scolded. 'Come onnnn! You know I'm sorry! You know I'm a good kid at heart! Here's a list of awesome things I've done since yesterday.' I held my palm out and extended a finger for everything in my list. 'I fed some stray cats. I helped an old lady find her car keys – it doesn't matter that she was my mum, it still counts! I held the door open for some cute girls. I let that Davian kid borrow my mechanical pencil even though I fully knew he wasn't going to give it back! I ate *all* of my vegetables last night for dinner, and *you know* that vegetables are one of my worst enemies! I *didn't* get into an argument with the comic shop salesperson about how ninjas *wouldn't* stand a chance in a zombie apocalypse because he *clearly* wasn't thinking straight since his parents kicked him out of their basement! And I showed up to school early today so I could help you!'

Zoe frowned. 'A real hero doesn't need to take credit for every good thing they do. That makes you sound like you're doing good things because you want people to say how great you are.'

'Fiiiiiine,' I whined. 'I'm sorry!'

'Your apology won't mean anything if you get into a huff right now,' Zoe said.

'Okay,' I replied, hanging my head low. I couldn't help but smile. 'You're right, okay? Happy? I *should've* helped you and I was a butthead for saying no.'

Zoe wagged her finger at me. 'I wouldn't have cared if you'd just said no. Instead you lied and told me you didn't want your *nap* to get interrupted!'

I chuckled. 'Yes, you're right about that too.'

'Is that funny to you?' Zoe asked, glaring at me.

I decided to be honest. 'C'mon, it's a *little* funny.'

Zoe stared at me for another second. Her eyes looked cold and mechanical, but suddenly she burst out laughing. 'Fine,' she said, coughing through her laugh. 'It might be a *little* funny.'

I set my book bag on the table next to us and scanned the room. 'Is there anything I can do to help right now?'

Zoe picked up her clipboard and read through her notes, silently moving her head back and forth with each new line on her task sheet. 'I think Gavin still needs some help—'

'Wait,' I said. Something had caught my eye at the far corner of the cafeteria. It moved so quickly that it was a black and white blur.

Zoe set her clipboard down. 'What is it?'

And then I saw it. The penguin had hopped down from the stage and stood out in the open. It was Hotcakes.

My body went from zero to sixty in about three seconds as I sprinted across the room.

'Chase!' Zoe shouted. '*What* are you doing?'

The penguin snapped its attention at me as I ran toward it. Spinning around, it started waddling to the long bench with the scaffolding above it. I don't know what you've heard about penguins, but those little birds are *fast*. Faster than I'd expected.

The other kids gasped as I ran. Gavin shouted something from behind me, but I couldn't tell what it was. I was too focused on catching the penguin.

The bird dashed along the wall, flapping its pointless wings in the air. I responded smoothly, cutting a curve across the middle of the room. He wasn't going to get away again if I had anything to do with it!

Hotcakes made it to the long bench under the scaffolding, hopping onto it in one bounce. Racing across the cafeteria, I watched him jump onto one of the metal rungs of the scaffolding. And then he slipped, falling against the wooden bench and flopping to the floor. He jumped back to its feet and started waddling again.

'Don't you move!' I shouted.

I was only about a metre and a half away when I dropped to my side and slid along the ground like I was sliding for first base. The penguin stopped in its tracks and faced me. He opened his beak and screamed like a banshee. I'm not embarrassed to say it freaked me out enough that I broke from my slide, kicking my feet along the polished floor and covering my face.

I smashed into the long wooden bench. The scaffolding above the bench tilted back and forth until the wooden plank at the top flipped onto its side. The paintbrushes and rollers that were on the board crashed to the floor next to me. A heavily braided rope swung back and forth from the scaffolding to a dark spot backstage where it disappeared. The rope had pink and green threads sewn into it.

My eyes followed the rope from backstage all the way to the plank where it was tied to one of the corners. Thankfully, the plank itself didn't fall off. I rolled onto my stomach, staring across the floor. There was no sign of the penguin.

I saw Zoe staring at me. Gavin was right behind her, laughing. Defeated, I lowered my face onto the cold floor.

'Ya done?' Gavin asked. He stepped into my field of vision, blocking my view of the rest of the cafeteria.

'Is Hotcakes gone?' I asked behind my palms.

Gavin took a knee on the floor. 'That thing was gone before you hit the bench. It ran right back into the air vent.'

'Chase! Are you okay?' Faith asked as she jogged up to me.

'I'm fine,' I said, standing. 'I'm just upset the penguin got away.'

Zoe approached, looking upset. 'Nice one,' she snipped, pointing at the paintbrushes and rollers on the floor. 'You seem to make a mess of things everywhere you go, don't you?'

Here I thought she was going to praise me for trying to catch the penguin. I huffed an annoyed breath, but I kept my mouth shut.

Anything I said would've only made things worse. Instead, I stared at the plank of wood that had tipped over on top of the scaffolding.

Zoe marched away and shouted more orders into her walkie-talkie about how there was another accident that needed fixing in the cafeteria. Faith smiled at me, letting me know that she wasn't mad. Gavin was staring at the air vent the penguin had used to escape.

My eyes drifted across the broken painting supplies as I nudged them with my foot. Looking back at the plank, I noticed the paint cans on the end of it. I don't know how I didn't notice it before, but they were all tipped sideways too, still attached to the wooden board with the braided rope dangling off the side. Wow. Thank goodness those paint cans hadn't fallen or else this whole thing would've been much worse.

I grabbed the handle of one of the cans and pulled, but it didn't budge. My fingers slipped and the handle popped back into place.

'What the…' I whispered. Then I saw that

the cans had been attached to the plank with nails around their base. Why would anyone nail paint cans down?

Gavin heard me. 'What's the matter?'

Tapping the plank, I said, 'These cans are nailed to the plank.'

Gavin reached up and slid his finger along the base of one of the cans. 'Man, you're one lucky duck,' he said. 'If these cans had been open, I'm pretty sure Zoe would never speak to you again.'

'That's weird, right?' I asked.

'Sure is,' Gavin said, turning toward me. 'Bell's about to ring. Meet before lunch? We still have to ask Eli about yesterday.'

'Sure,' I said, glancing at the clock just in time to see it tick over and hear the bell ring.

Gavin walked to the door but turned and said, 'Eli won't be in the cafeteria though. He's one of those straight-A students who spend lunch working in the library, so we'll have to look in there today. Grab Brayden before we go.'

'Brayden?' I asked. 'Why?'

'He's a monster expert, right?'

I nodded.

Gavin smiled. 'Library's fulla zombies. We'll need his help for this one.'

I stood still in the middle of the cafeteria as students left the room. I think my ears were trying to convince my brain that I had actually heard Gavin correctly.

Did he really just say something about zombies?

**Tuesday.
Gym class.**

I stood on the sidelines in gym class. Coach
Cooper said that the teams had been picked for
the entire week so I was going to be stuck with
the ridiculous moose costume for the next few
days. You'd think he'd rotate another student
out so that I could get in a game or two, but
he just sat near the entrance of the gymnasium,
sipping his half-lemonade-half-tea drink.

I guess I couldn't complain too much.
Keeping me in the mascot costume was a good
way to stay out of trouble since apparently,
trouble was looking for me.

'Anyone see that dweeb, Chase?' Jake hollered from the football field.

Several kids shook their heads. Brayden made sure to keep his eyes on the field rather than risk giving me away by sneaking a peek at me. I heard a few others comment on the fact that they had no idea there was even a 'Chase' in their gym class.

'That kid's so afraid of you that he's not even coming out to the field!' one of the boys in Jake's wolf pack said.

'It's not his fault,' Jake replied. 'He's just afraid of sports, like a true nerdling.'

Jake laughed at his own joke. His wolf pack took that as their sign to laugh too.

Once the game got started, it was easier for me to chill a little. After a few touchdowns from Jake's team, they were so satisfied with the lead that they stopped asking about where I was.

After an embarrassing turnover, Brayden's team had the ball. I'm not much of a sports guy, but at least I knew when a team was winning or losing. At that moment, Brayden's team was losing. Bad.

I watched as a short kid on Brayden's team hiked the ball. The quarterback snatched it and took a few steps back, searching for someone, anyone, to throw it to. I heard Brayden's voice from down the field and I looked over to see that he was completely out in the open.

Turning my huge mascot head, I started jumping up and down, pointing at Brayden. The quarterback chucked the ball so hard that it wobbled through the air. Time seemed to stand still as the ball floated through space, until finally…

Jake jumped like a lion going after its prey. Snatching the ball with one hand, he sailed into Brayden, smashing against him. Brayden looked like a ragdoll as he fell to the ground. I could see the pain on his face.

Jake jogged back to his goal line and into the end zone, scoring another six points for his team. His wolf pack ran circles around Brayden, laughing while he sat on the ground, rubbing his hurt knees.

It was awful and I was starting to feel my

anger swell up from deep within my stomach, but I knew I couldn't do anything without starting *something*.

Jake danced in the end zone for what seemed like an hour. He kept pointing two fingers in the air as he tapped his knees together over and over and over… and over.

I jogged to the end of the field, behind the goal post, and watched as Brayden's team helped him up. A few of my ninja clan were on his team, and it was good to see them by his side too.

After a moment, Jake's team set up for the kick-off as Brayden's team took their place at the other end of the field. A tall boy from the wolf pack ran at full speed towards the football He booted the ball so hard it flew all the way across the field, past the halfway line, past Brayden's team, past the goal post…

…and directly at me.

I froze, watching the brown come closer and closer. My normal response to an inflated leather ball coming at me at a hundred kilometres an hour was to flinch and dive to the ground, but for some reason I didn't do that. Instead, I held my arms out, catching the ball perfectly with the hairy moose gloves on my hands.

'Go!' Brayden cried.

I looked up through the eyeholes in my mask. All I could hear was my breath as it turned into quick gasps inside the mask. It sounds like it might've been cool, but it was more like something out of a scary movie.

I didn't have to think about it anymore my legs starting booking it. I guess they decided they were going to try and score a touchdown.

'Get him!' Jake shouted from the other end of the field. '*Get that moose!*'

So there I was – a kid in an oversized moose mask running straight into a team of students who wanted to tackle me.

The wolf pack was close enough that I could smell their cheap body spray. I wanted to brace for impact, but my legs had something else in mind.

Something *ninja*.

As soon as the first kid
dove at me, I jumped into the air, spinning
around so I faced the opposite direction. Sailing
over his head, I laughed as I completed the turn,
landing on my feet at full speed. I clutched the
ball closer to my side and leaned into my sprint.
Oh yeah, this was going to be *fun*.

Two other kids ran right at me. The first one
dove, but before he caught me, I dug my foot
into the dirt and spun a circle clean around
him. The other boy reached his arms out. I felt
his fingers slide against the moose mask so I
dipped my head down, slipping free from his
grip, spinning circles like crazy, trying to

confuse him. I didn't have to worry about him after that. He fell face first into the ground.

I steadied myself as the world spun outside my moose mask. I had to keep running. If I stopped long enough, someone from Jake's team was sure to tackle me.

Feeling a little dizzy, I ran as fast as I could toward the end zone. Most of the kids on Jake's team had stopped running after me, letting me pass by with almost no effort at all. It was like they had given up because I was too fast for them!

'*Stop him!*' I heard another voice shout.

I took that as my hint to run even faster. My legs burned as I pushed myself to score for Brayden's team. Sneaking a glance to my left, I could see the lines in the football field counting down as a sportscaster shouted in my mind.

'*He's at the forty! The thirty! The twenty! The ten!*'

And then Brayden's voice cut through. 'You're going the wrong way!'

I looked over my shoulder to see Brayden and his team staring at me. Jake and his team were on the other side of the field, laughing. I tried to stop, but it was impossible because of how fast I was going.

'Touchdown!' Jake shouted.

I slowed to a stop, letting the football drop into the grass.

At that moment, Coach Cooper's air horn went off, signalling for all the students to return to the locker rooms to get changed.

'Nice,' Brayden said.

I didn't say anything, too embarrassed to defend myself.

Our classmates all ran past us, desperate to change out of their gym clothes. Jake and his wolf pack laughed at me when they walked by. If they knew who it was under the mask, I'm sure their taunting would've been harsher. Brayden and I were the last ones on the field, So I took off the moose mask.

'Dude, I'm sorry about that.'

Brayden squinted, looking at the sky.

I wasn't sure if he was angry or sad. 'Dude?'

Suddenly, he burst out laughing. Wiping the

tears from his eyes, he spoke through quick gasps. 'You totally scored for the wrong team! I thought that sort of thing only happened in movies!'

I smiled, relieved. 'I guess not,' I said, chuckling.

'No,' Brayden said. 'You *really* stuffed up out there! Like, it was going awesome and cool up until you spun around in a million circles!'

I scratched the back of my neck. 'Yeah, not sure what I was thinking with that one.'

Brayden continued to laugh. 'And then you started running straight back to where you came from! And like, running *harder* than you were before! You were *determined* to score!'

I started feeling embarrassed again. 'Yeah, funny,' I said, biting my lip.

'Sorry, man,' Brayden said, smearing his hand across his tear-soaked cheek. 'It's just that was the funniest thing I've seen all year. My *cheeks* hurt! Thanks for the laugh.'

I put my hand on his shoulder and squeezed. 'No problem, man.'

Brayden stretched his arms out and sighed, catching his breath. 'So what's up?' he asked as he headed back toward the locker rooms.

'Gavin said he needs your help. Well, *we* need your help.'

'Anything for my ninja leader,' Brayden said jokingly.

'We have a lead on a suspect,' I said. 'Someone named Eli that might know something about the broken stage yesterday.'

'Okay,' Brayden said, nodding.

'Gavin said he's a straight-A student, so he'll in the library during lunch, studying or something. You'll need to meet us outside the cafeteria before lunch starts.'

Brayden stopped in his tracks. 'Free period in the library during lunch?' he whispered.

'Yeah,' I said. 'Zoe does sometimes.'

'*Zombies*,' Brayden whispered.

I paused, surprised. 'Gavin said the same thing!'

Brayden nodded, his eyes wide open, staring at me. 'He's right,' he said, jogging away from me. 'You guys are gonna need my help!'

I threw my arms in the air. 'Really? You're just gonna say, 'zombies', and run off with no explanation whatsoever?'

Brayden pulled open the gymnasium door and went inside.

I stuffed the moose gloves into the mask and trudged back to school. Lunch was coming up, so whatever Gavin and Brayden were talking about would be cleared up soon.

There was no way Buchanan School had zombies walking around, right? Zombies only existed in movies and video games, didn't they?

I realised that in that moment, I wasn't sure.

 **Tuesday. Lunch.**

Before finding Gavin and Brayden, I thought I'd pay my ninja clan another visit. All the talk of zombies in the library had me on edge, so I wanted to refocus my thoughts on something more realistic. But of course, Buchanan School had something else in mind.

As I turned the corner in the hallway, I saw my ninja clan standing outside the training room, grumbling about something.

'Hey, guys,' I said. 'What gives? How come you're out here and still in your street clothes?'

Naomi pointed at the door. 'Because of *him*.'

A lump formed in my throat as I looked through the window in the door. On the other side was Wyatt and a girl.

Suddenly the door whipped open and Wyatt flinched, acting surprised that we were in the hallway. 'Oh, excuse me,' he said unpleasantly. 'Had no idea anyone was out here.'

'What're you doing with this room?' I snipped.

'This?' Wyatt asked, turning in a circle. 'Oh, I saw that the school had an empty room, so I decided it'd be a great place to train my...*hall monitors.*'

'That's baloney, and you know it,' I shouted, angry.

The girl stepped into view and stood at Wyatt's side, holding his hand. It was Olivia Jones, the girl who tried to destroy the science fair two weeks ago. She smiled smugly as she chewed on a bright green piece of gum. The air was filled with spearmint-scented evil.

'Trouble, babe?' Olive asked Wyatt.

I coughed. '*Babe?*'

'You haven't heard?' Wyatt asked. 'Olive and I are going out now.'

'I'm in like with him,' Olive said.

'Gross,' I whispered, noticing the red band on her wrist.

Olive lifted her hand to show off her new bracelet. 'Like it? I earned it two weeks ago when Wyatt found out that it was *me* who tried to sabotage the science fair.'

Wyatt grinned. 'Looks like she's the first lady *and* a red ninja.'

'The first lady?' Naomi asked. 'But how? Don't you need to be the president's wife to have that position?'

Wyatt explained. 'The rules say if the president

isn't married, which Sebastian obviously *isn't*, then the position of first lady goes to his niece.' Wyatt gave us the best angry eyes he could. 'Now get lost before I send you all to the principal's office. In case you forgot, I'm the captain of the hall monitors.'

Naomi snapped. She balled her fists and held them out to Wyatt. 'That does it! This ends here and now!'

Wyatt stepped in front of Olive and held his open palm out as if he were inviting someone to fight him. His face was cool and collected, which made him more eerie.

I had to push against the rest of my ninja clan as they tried moving forward. Grabbing Naomi's elbow, I did my best to remain calm. 'No! *Not* like this! This is *exactly* what he wants!'

'Then I say let's give it to him!' Naomi said, pulling her arm free from my grasp. 'It's not like he doesn't deserve it!'

'It's not our place to decide what he deserves and what he doesn't!' I said, surprised at my own insight. 'The first rule of our ninja clan is that we *don't* fight! Have you all forgotten this?'

'Then what's the point of being in a ninja clan?' Wyatt laughed.

'Honour,' I said immediately. 'Doing the right thing. And right now, the right thing to do is walk away…even if I don't want to.'

Wyatt pointed down the hall. 'So go already! Get lost 'cause you're a bunch of losers on the *losing* side.'

I had to bite my lip to keep from saying anything else. I stared at Wyatt for a few more seconds, angry as heck, but I finally made myself take a breath. I felt the same way as the rest of my ninja clan. But I was their leader, and I had to act as one even if it meant feeling defeated in doing the right thing, which is actually the opposite of the truth. My victory came from doing the *right* thing, so why did I feel so bad about it?

I swallowed my pride and walked away. My ninja clan stood in front of Wyatt for a few seconds, but eventually followed me down the hall. Wyatt and Olive stayed in the hallway in front of the open door. I'm sure that as soon as the hall was clear, the red ninjas would come out to train in that room.

'We're without a home,' Naomi grunted with her arms folded.

Glancing at Naomi, I said, 'We are, but it's not the first time this has happened, and we'll bounce back just like we did last time.' I turned the corner and saw Gavin and Brayden waiting for me in the lobby. 'I've got some other business to attend to. Take a break today, alright? Get some lunch, drink some orange juice, eat a biscuit and laugh a little. It's not the end of the world.'

Naomi smiled and nodded. The rest of my ninja clan chuckled a little too. Things were bad, but we've been through worse, and I was positive that this little speed bump wasn't going to stop us from finding a place to train.

**Tuesday.
The library.**

Gavin and Brayden were in the middle of a conversion about the best way to deal with the library situation. Brayden had the idea of taking it slow so nobody would notice us. Gavin thought running at full speed was a better idea.

'Okay,' I said, leaning against the tinted glass walls of the cafeteria. 'Zombies. Explain it. *Now.*'

Gavin paused, darting his eyes at Brayden. 'You want to explain this, mister monster expert?'

Brayden didn't hesitate. 'Gladly,' he said, gesturing toward the library with his hands.

'The kids in there are Buchanan's best of the best. They're the straight-A students, and as most people know, straight-A students are allowed to use their lunch to study in the library if they want to.'

'Right,' I said, nodding. 'So?'

'Let me finish,' Brayden said, holding his hand up. 'The school assumes the smart kids will use their free period in the library to further their education by doing extra study or research. In theory, it's great because it would allow those kids to finish their homework early, and use the library's tools to help them.'

I nodded, trying to keep up. Brayden was speaking so fast and he sounded like some kind of university professor. 'So what about the zombies?'

Brayden smiled. 'The school has given these kids unlimited access to the wi-fi during this free period. They're allowed to use the internet for any kind of research they need, and if they have smart phones, they're allowed to use their phone's web browser too.'

'So what?' I asked, still confused.

'So,' Gavin said, 'those kids ain't usin' the internet for research! They're usin' it to update their statuses and send texts!'

Brayden put his hand on the library door. 'They're brainless zombies, staring at their phones. All of them.'

'That's *not* a zombie,' I said, relieved that there weren't actually undead monsters in the library.

Brayden pulled the door open. 'We'll see,' he said, stepping in. 'Stay close and keep your mouth shut.'

GAVIN   ME   BRAYDEN

I let Gavin go in front of me so I was the last in line. The cold air from the library hit me like a wall. The rest of the school was heated during the colder months of the year, but for some reason, the library had its air conditioning going at full blast. The other thing that surprised me was how abnormally silent it was.

On the wall to the side of us were the typical motivational posters with kittens hanging onto clotheslines, and shadows of people reading books. I saw more posters of Hotcakes.

Gavin took the lead and whispered. 'Eli will probably be somewhere in the back.'

'How do you know?' I asked.

'Zoe said she's seen him in here a few times,' Gavin replied. 'She noticed because she's the only kid whose eyes aren't glued to her phone.'

'I'm not surprised,' I said.

The three of us walked farther into the library. It was two stories, with an exposed staircase in the centre of the room. Surrounding the staircase were several rectangular tables, with a student seated at each one of its four sides.

The lighting in the massive room was different from anywhere else in the school. Instead of harsh fluorescent lights, there were soft yellow lights, casting the room in a warm glow.

And then I finally understood what Brayden meant when he said that kids were zombies. Every kid in the room was breathing through their mouth and staring into a phone they held with both hands about five centimetres from their face.

You know when you walk outside at night and all you hear are the sound of crickets? Well, it was a lot like that, but instead of cricket chirps, there were short vibration alerts and random *ting!* sounds.

Brayden inched his way forward. 'Don't make any sudden movements,' he whispered. 'If you do, they'll see you.'

'What happens if they see us?' I asked.

'You don't want to know,' he replied.

As we walked down the aisle, I could see the faces of the zombies seated at their desks. Their mouths were open and their faces glowed with the light from their phone screens. I had to smile because it looked a lot like the area in a video game shop where kids were allowed to play demo games. Next time you're in one of those shops, check it out and you'll see what I mean. Every single person playing has their neck craned backward and their mouth open as they stare at the screen.

Just as we were at the staircase, my foot nudged one of the desk legs. It wasn't hard, but it was enough to cause the four zombies seated at the table to drop their phones.

'Dude, are you nuts?' Brayden whispered harshly, but it was too late. The zombies had already seen us.

'*Whuuuuuuuut…*' one of the zombies groaned. She flopped her hand on the table until she found her phone again. She held it in the air and pointed the screen at me. She had been watching a video of a kitten that was trying to jump out of a box. '*Waaaaaaatch this cuuuuuute videeeeeeooooo.*'

'Run!' Brayden shouted.

At that instant, every zombie in the room looked up from the phones, squinting so their eyes could adjust. With open mouths, they all started groaning about how we needed to watch whatever cute animal video was on the phone.

Gavin took off, sliding over one of the tables. 'C'mon, Chase!'

I didn't waste any time, rolling across the surface of the same table. The zombies at the desk pointed their phones at me, grumbling about their status updates. I kept my eyes focused on the lights in the ceiling, trying not

to catch of glimpse of one of those kitten
videos. I'm a ninja at heart, but who *wouldn't*
want to watch a cute video like that?

The zombies stood up and hobbled towards
us. Their legs must've fallen asleep because they
were clumsy, trying to keep their balance and
stumbling into each other.

'Eli's back here!' Gavin said, jogging between
the tall bookshelves. He paused, looking past
me. 'Where's Brayden?'

I stopped running and spun in place. The
zombies weren't following us, and I could see

why. They were all gathering around Brayden as he covered his eyes.

'Go on without me!' Brayden cried. 'I'm done for! The videos! They're too cute to pass up! Go! I'll find you after lunch! *Gooooooo...!*' his voice trailed off. The last thing I heard him say was, '*That kitty's never gonna fit in that tube! Cute little kitty!*'

Brayden had become a zombie. I mean, y'know... at least until *after* lunch.

Gavin finally made it to one of the rooms in the back. Along the wall was a series of doors about two metres apart. Each led to a small study room with a desk and a power outlet. There was a student inside each room. Eli was in the last one.

I peered through the glass door and saw his phone's screen. It looked like he was shopping for one of those oversized magician's hats – the kind where a bunny goes in but doesn't come out.

Gavin swung the door open and stepped inside. Eli looked up from his phone and flinched, scooting his chair back until it bumped his desk, but with Gavin and I blocking his exit, he was completely trapped.

ELI →

Eli was dressed in all-black clothing and wearing eyeliner. His black jeans were baggy enough that three people could've easily fit inside them. Drops of orange paint were splattered at the bottom of his jeans. He stared at us from behind his long greasy fringe.

'You seem a tad jumpy,' Gavin said with his cowboy accent.

'Maybe because you two barged into my study room,' Eli said, pushing his hair behind his ears.

'What do you know about yesterday's accident in the cafeteria?'

'I wasn't in lunch yesterday,' Eli said, angry. 'I'm always in here during lunch.'

'Not at lunch,' Gavin said. 'Yesterday *morning* when Sophia's penguin was set free.'

'Oh that,' Eli whispered. After a second, he said, 'It was *awesome*, and frankly, I'm glad the penguin escaped his caged life! No animal should have to live like a prisoner.'

'Interesting perspective,' Gavin said. 'So you think it's a good thing that Hotcakes got loose?'

Eli snickered. 'Who names a penguin Hotcakes?'

Gavin ignored the question. 'Rumour has it you were around the cage,' Gavin said.

'Everyone was around that cage,' Eli said. 'There was a *penguin*.'

Gavin stuck his tongue out of the side of his mouth and scratched more notes onto his notepad.

Finally, Eli broke the silence. 'Oh I get it. You think *I* did it? Well, you're completely wrong about that, *good sirs*. I didn't have anything to do with the penguin or anything else for that matter!'

I folded my arms. 'Is there any information

you could tell us that might help us find the kid who did it? What did you see yesterday?'

Eli mocked me, folding his arms and leaning back in his chair. 'I already told you I didn't do it, so we're done here.'

Gavin sighed. 'What about the kid in the hockey mask? Play any hockey lately, Eli? Hmm?'

'If by hockey, you mean hacky sack, then yeah, I've been playing a ton recently,' Eli said.

'No,' Gavin said, rubbing his eyebrows. 'That's not what I meant.'

'Are you guys, like, the school detectives now? You can't just burst into my study period and demand answers from me, y'know. I have my rights and I want to speak to the principal.'

Gavin held his open palms out. 'Easy now, cupcake. I just wanted—'

'*Don't* call me *cupcake*,' Eli said.

Gavin took a breath.

Eli slid forward on his chair, looking uneasy. 'Fine, look, I saw some kid hanging around Sophia's penguin yesterday morning, alright?'

'Why didn't you say something before?'

Gavin asked, straightening his posture, scribbling again on his notepad.

Eli ran his fingers through his hair. 'I don't know,' he said with a high-pitched voice. 'Maybe 'cause you two spooked me or something. Anyway, the kid you want to ask is Calvin. I saw him poking around that cage.'

Gavin wrote the name on his notepad and circled it. 'Sophia said something about him too.'

'There ya go,' Eli said, sitting back. 'Find *that* guy.'

'Who is he?' I asked. 'I've never heard of him before.'

Eli glared at me. 'Who are *you*?' he asked with attitude. 'I've been going to this school since kindergarten, and I've never seen *you* before. Just 'cause you haven't seen someone doesn't mean they aren't real. You think the school revolves around you or something?'

Ouch. I lowered my gaze, embarrassed.

'Alright, alright,' Gavin said. 'So where exactly did you see Calvin?'

Eli shook his head and blinked slowly. 'I dunno, backstage, I guess? I mean I was backstage, I think? I don't know. Everything was pretty crazy when it all went down. Actually, I think I was over by the bench against the wall.'

'That's where the penguin was,' I said.

'Was it?' Eli asked, confused and scratching his arm. 'That's right, I *was* back by the stage. I was checking out some of the backdrops that were being painted.'

'Painting?' I asked. 'Were *you* painting?'

'No,' Eli replied. 'Why?'

I almost mentioned the paint cans that had been nailed to the scaffold, but I stopped myself. 'No reason. I just uh…' I pointed at his jeans. 'I just noticed some orange paint on your jeans.'

'Oh, dude!' Eli said, rolling his eyes. 'My mum's gonna kill me for getting paint on these!'

'Maybe watch where you step next time, huh?' I laughed.

At that moment, the bell rang, signalling the end of lunch. The zombies in the library all shook their heads, returning to normal. Eli snatched his book bag off the floor and hoisted it onto his back.

'This conversation is over,' Eli grunted. 'If you come near me again, I swear I'll go straight to Principal Davis and tell him you were messing with me.'

Gavin stepped aside from the door. 'Thank you for your time,' he said politely.

I watched Eli walk away. When he was gone, I turned back to Gavin. 'So he's innocent?' I sighed. 'What a waste of time.'

'Not true,' Gavin said, scribbling in his notepad. 'We got a location out of him. He said he was backstage.'

'Okay?' I said sarcastically. 'That doesn't mean anything.'

'It's just another thing to check out, ain't it?' Gavin said. 'If we're investigating this, then we should investigate *all* of it, right?'

'Right,' I said reluctantly. It wasn't that I didn't want to find Calvin – it was that I didn't want to waste more time checking out a lead that didn't matter.

'Meet me in the morning before school?' Gavin asked. 'We'll check out the backstage during homeroom and see if we can find anything back there.'

I nodded. 'Until then,' I sighed.

Gavin must not have heard the sarcasm in my voice, or if he did then he didn't care. He patted me on the shoulder and walked towards the exit of the library.

Eli ended up having nothing to do with the talent show disaster, that much was obvious, but I had to remind myself that at least we were getting a direction. Who knows, maybe Gavin was right, and there was something worth investigating backstage. If anything, all this work was a nice distraction from whatever Wyatt was up to, and for me, a distraction like that was worth a thousand bucks.

Sophia and Eli had both mentioned Calvin. Gavin and I had never heard of the kid. Whoever he was, he was beginning to look like someone that we *needed* to question because from what Sophia and Eli had said, he was there when Hotcakes was set free.

**Wednesday.
The cafeteria.**

The bell rang just as I stepped into the cafeteria.
There were still two days left to set up for the
talent show. Zoe had convinced Principal Davis
to host the talent show during the first half of
the school day on Friday so everyone would
have to miss their morning classes. Nobody
complained about it because it was an awesome
idea. I suspect even the teachers thought it
would be a nice break from the normal routine
of handling a roomful of loud students.

'Over here, Chase,' Gavin said, standing next
to my cousin and Faith.

Zoe looked up at me and smiled. When I approached her, she put her arms around me and gave me a hug.

'What's that for?' I asked.

'It's because I hate being mad at you,' Zoe said. 'I'm still not happy with you, but I'm not mad anymore.'

'It's a start,' I said, smiling.

'Have you guys heard of someone named Calvin?' Gavin asked, pulling his notepad from his pocket and flipping it open.

Zoe crinkled her nose. 'Hmmm,' she hummed. 'The kid who stole the time capsule that one time?'

'No, that's Brody,' Faith said. 'And I think he was cleared of those charges – something about being framed and whatnot.'

'She's right,' I said. 'That's Brody Valentine. I actually know him. I don't think he'd do anything as vicious as breaking a stage or anything like that.'

'That's right,' Zoe said, nodding. 'Then I don't know anyone named Calvin.'

'Sophia and Eli *both* said they saw Calvin messing around with the cage before Hotcakes got free,' Gavin said.

Faith snorted, and then covered her mouth instantly. 'Hotcakes is the name of the penguin? I *like* it.'

Gavin ignored her comment. He turned to Zoe and said, 'Did you see anyone by the penguin's cage that morning?'

Zoe hummed, thinking as her eyes glazed over. 'I couldn't tell you,' she said. 'I was so distracted by a bunch of other stuff.'

Faith jumped up and sat on the tabletop

next to us, resting her arms on her knees. 'You think Calvin might be the kid in the hockey mask?'

I raised my eyebrows. 'Maybe. We just don't know for sure yet.'

'No leads except for someone named Calvin, huh?' Faith asked.

'Not a single one,' I replied. 'On the bright side, we know that Olive and Wyatt are dating now.'

'*No way!*' Faith said. 'That's a recipe for disaster if I've ever heard one. That's as bad as squeezing lemon into your eyes after cutting onions!'

'It's as bad as getting a paper cut on your eyeball!' Gavin said, cringing.

Zoe chimed in. 'It's as bad as a ninja who punched themselves in the face because they thought they were quick enough to dodge their own attack.'

Gavin laughed. 'It's as bad as a ninja who forgot their uniform at home so they had to borrow their mum's leggings!'

'Oh good,' I said sarcastically. 'We're making fun of me again.'

All three of my friends laughed. A huge smile was plastered on Zoe's face, which made me happy.

'We make fun of you 'cause you're our friend,' she said. 'Come on, lighten up. We all do it to each other.'

I smiled, knowing she was right. Then I tried to make a joke myself. 'It's as bad as tipping a cow over while it sleeps!'

My friends gasped, horrified.

'Whoa, major burn on cows, dude!' Gavin said, upset.

Zoe jumped up, angry. 'Yeah, man. Why would anyone ever do that to a cow? Are you some kind of monster or something?'

'What'd a cow ever do to you?' Faith asked, disappointed.

'Serious?' I asked, watching Zoe and Faith walk away. 'It was a joke! I heard people used to do that for fun! I would never do that to a cow! I *love* cows!'

'Can't win 'em all,' Gavin said.

'Whatever,' I said. 'Let's just get backstage and see if we can figure out who the kid in the hockey mask is.'

Several minutes later, Gavin and I were digging around the backstage of the cafeteria. It was spooky how often I'd been back there since I started at this school. It was almost like evil grew from somewhere around there.

Gavin scanned the floor, searching for anything that would be useful. I pushed my hands in my pockets as I hobbled down the narrow passage. There was so much junk and boxes filled with random things that it was almost impossible to walk freely.

I stepped over the thick braided rope with the hot-pink and green threads that I saw the other day. The rope ran down the narrow corridor and out into the cafeteria. Apparently it was still attached to the scaffolding.

'We're never gonna find anything back here,'

I said, pushing the rope aside with my foot.

'You don't know that,' Gavin replied. 'The worst thing you can do is *not* help.'

'I'm helping!' I said defensively. 'Who said I wasn't helping?'

'You're standin' around pouting!' Gavin said. 'Make yourself useful and look for something, *anything*, that doesn't belong!'

'This place is filled with random junk!' I said. '*Nothing* belongs back here!'

'Then look for something that sticks out more than normal,' Gavin said, but stopped instantly. 'Did you hear that?'

I stopped in my tracks. 'Hear what?'

A faint tapping answered my question. *Clickety clickety clickety.*

'What was that?' I asked.

Gavin shrugged his shoulders. 'I'unno,' he grunted.

Clickety clickety clickety.

'There it is again!' Gavin said.

Clickety clickety clickety.

'It's getting closer,' I whispered, afraid.

Clickety clickety clickety clickety clickety clickety.

I stumbled backwards as the tapping sounds got closer and closer. The clicks were maddening and loud inside my head. It sounded like a monster tapping its claws on the floor.

And then came the sound that made me snap.

Squaaaaaaaaaawk!

I didn't stop to see what it was. I turned to run down the hall but stumbled over the boxes behind me. Several props from the drama club spilled to the floor, including all kinds of hockey masks. There must've been a dozen of them on the floor beside me.

I slid the masks around with my feet. The kid Gavin and I chased after must've got his mask from this box, which would make perfect sense since the scooters were stolen from the drama club too.

I looked back to see if Gavin noticed the masks, but I saw that he was already sprinting away in the other direction.

Squaaaaaaaaaawk!

My heart skipped a beat, remembering that a monster was after me. Pushing the hockey masks away from me, I rolled back to my feet and moved down the narrow passage. The tapping sounds were getting louder and sounded as if they were right behind me.

There was no way I was going to look back. I was too scared that I'd be frozen in fear at the sight of whatever it was that was chasing after me.

The passage grew darker as I ran further into it. The walls began to pinch together making me slow my escape and walk sideways. The tapping sound grew louder and faster as I moved slower and slower. It was like a terrible nightmare. Finally, I made it to the end of the corridor. A short stack of cardboard boxes were piled up in front of me, basically telling me I couldn't go any further. Clenching my jaw, I turned slowly to see my attacker.

The space in front of me was empty. The silence was now scarier than the tapping. I shut my eyes and took a deep breath, trying my hardest not to pass out from fear.

I opened my eyes, staring into space, allowing myself to see everything by focusing on nothing. It's a ninja technique where you stare into space and allow your peripheral vision to do what it does best, which is to see movement off to the side that you're not looking at.

The corridor was completely still as I took a step out.

And then a small black creature twitched in the shadows. I flinched, feeling my heart drop until I realised what it was I was looking at.

A few metres away was the missing penguin, staring at me with its head cocked sideways. If it could talk, it would've been like, 'Dude, what's *wrong* with you?'

Needless to say, I felt a little dumb for not realizing it was the penguin chasing me. In my defence, I was in a dark hallway and thought I was going to die.

Hotcakes hopped forward once and dropped something from his beak. A folded slip of paper landed gently on the floor. And then the he squawked once more before disappearing into an open air vent nearby.

I slid out from the spot I was hiding in. 'Someone should really fix all these open vents,' I whispered as I picked up the slip of paper. It was wet from the penguin's beak. When I unfolded it, I couldn't believe my eyes.

A,

The penguin plan didn't work out, but we have one more shot on Friday morning. I won't mess it up this time.

There wasn't a signature.

I studied the note for a moment. It must be referring to the talent show, but it was obvious that there was *more* going on than anyone

A,
The penguin plan didn't
work out, but we have one
more shot on Friday morning.
I won't mess it up this time.

suspected. It sounded like the penguin was only part of the equation. Was Gavin right? Could it have been a distraction so someone could wreck the stage?

'I won't mess it up this time,' I whispered, reading the note out loud.

Mess what up? Was it possible that they wanted to break more than just a corner of the stage? I felt sick.

Looking at the open air vent, I tightened my lips, thinking about how Hotcakes had dropped the note off. Was it on purpose? Was he trying to solve this mystery too? Could Brayden have been right? Are penguins smarter than everyone thought?

So many questions!

I heard footsteps close in on my position. When I looked over, I saw Gavin in the narrow passage.

'You okay?' he asked, but before I could answer, he said, 'It was the penguin, wasn't it? I realised it as soon as I jumped back into the cafeteria.'

I laughed. 'I realised the same thing as soon as I saw I couldn't run anymore.'

'Did he freak out at you?'

I shook my head, handing my friend the note. 'Nope, but he left me this.'

Taking the wet note in his hands, Gavin read it silently. 'It's addressed to 'A',' he said. 'Hotcakes left this for you?'

'I know, right? Weird,' I said, walking back to the cafeteria. 'Maybe Zoe will know who the note's for.'

A few minutes later Gavin and I were sitting at a table in the cafeteria. The room was completely empty since everyone had left for first period.

Zoe held the note, chewing on her lip the way she did when she was concentrating. 'A…' she whispered. Her eyes looked past the note and at me. 'You found this backstage?'

I scratched the back of my neck. 'Uh, yeah. I *found* it. Let's go with that.'

'Why's it wet?' Zoe asked, rotating the note in her hands.

I set my hands on the table and sighed. 'Hotcakes gave it to me.'

Immediately, Zoe dropped the note on the table. '*Ew! Seriously?* That was in the penguin's *mouth*?'

Gavin laughed. 'A little bit of penguin spit ain't gonna hurt ya.'

Zoe cocked an eyebrow. 'Um, have you heard of a little thing called bacteria? Actually, *millions* of little things that make up bacteria?' She stretched her fingers out in front of her as if she didn't want to risk touching anything. 'So gross, you guys. Seriously, *sick*.'

I put my hand over the note and slid it back to me. 'Do you know anyone who goes by A?'

Zoe pulled out an antibacterial wipe from her book bag and tore open the pack. I wasn't surprised to see that she carried something like that with her. Scrubbing her fingers with the wipe, she said, 'I don't know anyone who just goes by A, no. But I *do* know an *Adam* that works for me. He's one of the guys backstage. He helps guide kids through the back before and after their act. Adam's also in charge of making sure the curtain goes up and down when it needs to.'

Gavin sighed like an old cowboy as he stood from the table. 'Looks like this whole mess is messier than we thought.'

'It seems there's more going on here than just a penguin getting set free,' I said. 'It's beginning to look like it wasn't just a childish prank.'

Zoe frowned and started chewing her lip again. 'All I wanted to do was put on a talent show. I wanted to bring some fun to the school, and some jerk has to go and try to ruin things.'

I remained silent. Gavin didn't say anything either. He just reached across the table and set his hand on Zoe's. It must've helped because she smiled softly at him. *Gross.*

The three of us decided to meet back at the cafeteria before lunch. Adam was next on the list to question, even though we weren't a hundred per cent certain the note was addressed to him.

As I walked away from Gavin and Zoe, I felt a chill travel down my spine, just as I had when walking into school Monday morning. Bad things were happening at Buchanan, and my friends and I were smack dab in the middle of it.

**Wednesday.
Gym class.**

I was the last one out of the gymnasium and the
only one wearing a goofy-looking moose outfit.
The inside of the head was beginning to smell a
little funky from not being washed properly.
Why couldn't I have picked a cooler mascot
than a moose? Why not a knight? Or a Viking?
Man, why didn't I choose a super huge robot
instead? Total missed opportunity on my part.

Jake pointed and said some pretty insulting
stuff as I took my place on the sidelines. I tried
to play it off by clutching my belly and moving
my shoulders up and down like I was laughing.

'Hey, coach!' Jake shouted. 'We want that dumb moose on our team! Can we do that?'

Coach Cooper waved his hand with a huge grin from the gym doors. He obviously couldn't hear a word Jake was saying.

Jake pointed at me. 'If you feel like scoring another touchdown for us today, feel free, alright?'

I set one of my hands on my hips and wagged my finger at him like I was disagreeing. I felt like such an idiot.

Pacing back and forth next to the field, I watched Brayden's team get owned by Jake's. Every time Jake's team scored a touchdown, I made the mascot look like he was disappointed. Every time Brayden's team scored, I decided I'd jump up and down, doing a happy dance – too bad Brayden's team never scored.

As the game went on, I listened to the sound of my own breathing inside the mask. Since I wasn't doing anything and had nobody to talk to, I thought about the kid in the hockey mask. I took advantage of the fact that I had the whole period to sit and think inside the moose costume.

The penguin was set free before school on Monday, during the time that Zoe and her team began setting things up for the talent show. The penguin was part of an act in the show and was there on Monday morning because Zoe wanted all the acts to run through a rehearsal five days before the actual show.

While the penguin was running around, someone broke one of the corners of the stage that Gavin was building. Then they took off on a scooter stolen from the drama club, which was when I saw them. The kid was wearing a hockey mask, which turned out to be another prop from the drama club taken from one of their boxes backstage.

Zoe told us to speak to Sophia first, since it was her penguin. Sophia name-dropped Eli, but the only thing he was good for was telling us that he was working with the paint cans backstage. Sophia and Eli both mentioned someone named Calvin, who we haven't spoken to yet. Gavin and I have never even heard of the kid, so we're still trying to figure out who exactly he is.

After that, the penguin dropped the note from its little beak – the note that was addressed to 'A'. Zoe then told us someone named Adam works backstage for the talent show. I guess he's next on the list for us to question.

I blinked, returning to gym, surprised to see everyone staring at me. Jake's wolf pack was running at full speed in my direction. It was just like the day before except I wasn't holding…

I looked down and saw the football in my hands. I must've caught it when I was zoned out!

My ninja skills kicked in again without warning. If I had thought about it, I probably would've just dropped the ball because I didn't want to make a fool of myself again, but my legs were already running.

Jake's teammates dove at me again. The first few were easy to dodge. All I had to do was dig my foot into the grass to switch directions and they sailed right past me.

Three other kids stood between the end zone and me. I made sure to take a mental note about where the sun was just in case I got mixed up again. It was shining directly in front of me as I ran toward Jake and his team. I just had to keep running for the sun and I'd be fine.

The first kid threw her arms out, trying to tackle me. I arched my back and sped up as my moose helmet bobbed on my shoulders. I felt her fingers scrape against my side, but she couldn't grab hold of my shirt. She grunted as she hit the ground.

The second kid dipped his head down and barrelled toward me like a train, which if you had any ninja training, you'd know that was a huge mistake. All I had to do was step to the side as he ran by, rolling against his train motion. And that's exactly what I did. He ploughed into the field.

But I didn't stop. There was one last kid standing in my way – Jake, the leader of the wolf pack, and a member of Wyatt's red ninja clan.

I clenched my jaw and ran at full speed towards the end zone. Jake sprinted for me as I curved around him. I glanced at the sun one last time to make sure it was still in front of me. The blinding light reassured me that I was okay.

With huge strides, I ran into the end zone, scoring the only touchdown Brayden's team had scored all week. Applause erupted behind me as I lifted both hands in victory.

Suddenly, Jake slammed into me, tackling me to the ground. The grass and dirt burned my elbows as I slid against earth. My head bounced like a golf ball inside the moose helmet. Finally, I stopped, lying in the open grass and in the worst searing pain imaginable.

I squinted at the sun, but a shadow loomed over me, blocking out the light. It was Jake, staring at me through the eyes of the mask.

'So that's where you've been all week,' he said.

I tried to say something smart, but it came out as a painful groan.

Coach Cooper's air horn went off again, signalling the end of gym.

Jake glanced away, and then back to me. 'This isn't over, Chase. You embarrassed me out here today, and you'll get what's coming to you. Tomorrow. *Tomorrow.*'

Jake picked himself off the ground and jogged back to the locker rooms. Brayden helped me to my feet. I brushed the grass off myself and took the mask off. The cold air felt good against my smashed up face. Brayden and I made our way back to the locker rooms, joking about how much we hated gym class.

**Wednesday.
Lunch.**

The second I stepped out of the gym, Sophia
cornered me. She was hugging her textbooks
close to her body. 'Chase! Have you found
Hotcakes yet?'

I shook my head sadly. 'No, not yet, but
we're still trying.'

Sophia frowned. 'It's been two days.
Hotcakes has been on his own for *two days*!'

I could see the tears forming in her eyes. I
wasn't sure what to say. 'Uh, yeah. It's cool
though. I'm sure he's fine.'

Shaking her head, Sophia spoke softly. 'He's on his own and probably starving. I feel terrible for letting him out of my sight for even a second. It wasn't supposed to be like that!'

'No,' I said, shaking my head. 'You're right. We should've found him right after he escaped. I'm sorry that we haven't yet.'

Sophia looked up at me. Her eyes sparkled with tears. Biting her lower lip, she turned around and sped off. If this were a television show, I'd probably go after her, but since this was real life, I had no idea what to do.

She looked *so* sad and I felt awful.

After a few minutes, I met Gavin outside the cafeteria. He was standing with Zoe and Faith. They were cupping their hands on the tinted windows.

'Is he in there?' I asked as I approached them.

Zoe didn't move. Her breath was fogging up the glass in front of her face. 'Yeah, he's sitting with a bunch of his friends.'

Faith didn't look away from the glass either. 'He's kinda cute, isn't he?'

I cupped my hands on the glass and squinted through the window. Adam was toward the back of the room. He was dressed like a prepster, wearing a buttoned-up shirt, khaki pants, and brown loafers. His brown hair was slicked back, styled like one of those 1960s actors.

'Whatever, he's not *that* good looking,' I said, a little upset at Faith's comment.

Faith laughed. 'Jealous much?'

'Whatever,' I said, stepping away from the window. I pushed the door to the lunchroom wide open and marched inside.

Gavin hustled to keep up with me. 'Easy, tiger,' he said jokingly. 'I'm sure Faith didn't mean anything by that.'

I stopped in the middle of the aisle, standing in the way of a bunch of kids, making them walk around us. 'Just tell me what the plan is,' I said, unsure exactly why I was unhappy.

Gavin scratched his chin, carefully considering our options.

Adam was at one of the tables on the east side of the cafeteria, closest to the stage. He was sitting with members of the drama club. I recognised a few of the kids from one of the plays they had performed recently. Adam wasn't in the play, but even stagehands were considered part of the club.

The lunchroom felt empty again. It was weird to see half-filled tables as students were sprinkled across the cafeteria. Was there some sort of week-long field trip I wasn't aware of? Where'd everyone go?

Gavin took the lead as usual and approached the table. 'Play along, alright?'

'What's the plan, boss?' I asked.

'Good cop, bad cop,' Gavin replied.

'What's that?'

Gavin glanced over his shoulder at me. 'One of us acts really nice to the kid,' he explained. 'And then one of us acts like a jerk to him. It'll make it easier for Adam to talk to the good cop, hopefully spilling everything he knows about what happened on Monday. So when we get up there, I'll go first, okay?'

I nodded. Perfect. Gavin was going to be the cool nice guy while I had to figure out how to act bad. I'm not a mean kid at heart, but for some reason I actually *felt* angry with Adam. I don't know why because I've never talked to the kid in my life! And don't say it was because Faith said he was cute. I was already over that...I think.

As we approached the table, I overheard Adam saying, 'So yeah, that bike's gonna cost three hundred bucks, so I'll definitely get it. That'll leave me with a little extra for comic books.'

Gavin stopped at Adam's table and waited patiently for them to notice. When they did, he slapped the table with his open palm. The crack echoed across the noisy cafeteria, silencing half the students in the room.

'*Where were you on Monday morning?*' he shouted, pointing at Adam's face.

Adam flinched, scooting his chair away from

the table. His friends
looked at each other,
confused about the
angry kid standing
at their table.

ADAM

'What the— *What's your
deal, man?*' Adam growled.

'*Where were you?*' Gavin
shouted again.

I stood silently behind Gavin, balling my
fists, nervously waiting my turn.

Slapping the table again, Gavin spoke
through clenched teeth. '*Monday morning!
You'd better tell me before—*'

I took that as my cue. Stepping in front of
Gavin, I raised my hands and made them look
like claws. Darting my eyes back and forth,
I growled like a dinosaur as I tried to talk, but
since I wasn't sure what to say, I just said, '*I'm
crazy!*'

Everyone at the table laughed.

Gavin stepped backwards and looked at me,
puzzled. 'Dude, *what* are you doing?'

I turned my head the way I thought a dinosaur would. 'I'm doing the bad cop thing,' I hissed.

'No, *I'm* the bad cop,' Gavin snipped. 'You're the *good* cop!'

Adam sat forward and laughed heartily. 'You guys are trying to do good cop, bad cop? Looks more like bad actor cop, pterodactyl cop.'

I dropped my arms down to my side and stood straight. I know it was an insult, but I was too distracted by how awesome a pterodactyl cop would be.

Gavin sighed. 'Look, man. We just want to know where you were on Monday morning.'

'In here,' Adam said, looking around the cafeteria.

'What are you doing for the talent show?' Gavin asked.

'Nothing,' Adam replied. 'I'm just one of the stagehands. I'm backstage the entire time.'

'What do you know about Hotcakes?' I asked.

Adam shrugged his shoulder. 'I like 'em? Pancakes are my favourite thing for breakfast.'

'Hotcakes the *penguin*,' I said.

'Oh, that,' Adam replied nervously. He tapped at the table with his fingers. 'No clue.'

I took the note the penguin had dropped and set it on the table in front of him.

Adam's face remained unchanged as if he were a statue. 'Where'd you find that?'

'A friend gave it to me,' I said, smiling. 'You recognise it, don't you?'

Adam paused. His chest rose slowly as he took a breath. At last, he spoke. 'Whatever. You guys are pullin' my leg, aren't you? I wasn't anywhere near that penguin on Monday. Is that what you need to hear? I was backstage the entire time! I had nothing to do with the penguin or the busted stage or that kid that burst into the hallway in a hockey mask on a scooter.'

'He got the mask and scooter from the drama club boxes backstage,' I said. 'Did you see anyone poking around back there before Hotcakes was set free?'

Adam smirked. 'I saw a lot of kids poking

around backstage before that penguin got loose. It was rehearsal, so everyone was busy doing something.'

Adam had a point. Everyone helping with the talent show was probably busy, so someone could've easily set Hotcakes free without any witnesses.

I shut my eyes and pinched the bridge of my nose. When I looked at Gavin, I could tell he was frustrated too. The entire investigation had been one dead-end after another. The talent show was only two days away, and we were basically still at the starting line as far as figuring out who the kid in the hockey mask was.

The only real lead we had was a note addressed to someone named A. With as many 'A' names as there were at Buchanan, the odds were against us that Adam was even the right kid.

Adam pointed at me. 'You know who you need to ask? That Calvin kid. I'm pretty sure he was jostling that bird's cage on Monday.' Adam lifted his finger and tapped towards us as if he were pushing an imaginary button. 'And y'know what? Now that I think of it, I saw him messing with the drama club's stuff back there too! Yeah, he was playing with a hockey mask!'

Finally! A connection that meant something. If Adam had seen Calvin take the hockey mask from the back room, then that might've been enough to lead to the full truth. The only problem was that we still didn't know who Calvin was. My stomach turned, realizing that this new kid was definitely going to be a problem for us. He was going to be another bully in the sea of bullies at Buchanan School.

Gavin looked at me then back at Adam. '*Who's* Calvin? Is he in the cafeteria right now?'

Adam paused, blinking rapidly as he looked around the cafeteria. 'Calvin? He's about medium height, sorta gangly. Um...he's got short brown hair, brown eyes, wears a lot of T-shirt-and-jeans outfits.'

I rubbed my eyebrows, feeling a headache coming on. 'So he looks like every boy at this school,' I said.

Shrugging, Adam smiled tightly. 'What can

I tell ya? He looks like you. Oh, he's new here. Maybe that's why you haven't heard of him.'

I folded my arms, scanning the room for anyone who looked like the person Adam had described, but a lot of the students looked about the same height and body shape. This wasn't going to be easy.

'Actually, I think he had a white patch of hair on his head,' Adam added. 'Yeah, I remember seeing that and thinking it was weird.'

'It could be some kind of birthmark,' Gavin said, writing in his notepad. When he was finished, he flipped it shut and smiled gently at Adam. 'Thank you for your time.'

Adam tilted his head like he was wearing a hat to bid us farewell. 'Not a problem.'

The bell rang as Gavin and I walked towards the lunchroom doors. Zoe and Faith were waiting for us there.

'What'd you find out?' Zoe asked. 'Was he the one that did it?'

Gavin shook his head. 'No, but we we've got a solid lead.'

'Calvin came up *again*,' I said. 'But this time there was more. Adam said he saw Calvin messing around with the hockey masks backstage.'

Zoe clenched her fist. 'Got him!'

'So where is he?' Faith asked. 'What's he look like?'

Gavin jerked his thumb at me and laughed. 'Like him.'

'Har har,' I said. 'Calvin is supposedly the same height and weight as me. Brown hair, brown eyes, y'know, all that super handsome stuff.'

This time, Zoe faked a laugh. 'Har har.'

'He's got a birthmark in his hair though,' I continued. 'Adam said he saw a white patch of hair on the back of Calvin's head, so all we gotta do is find someone with a patch of white hair!'

'Great,' Faith sighed. 'In a school with a thousand students, finding one will be a piece of cake.'

Zoe laughed, looked at me and said, 'What if this was like one of your weird science-fiction movies? And *you* were Calvin, but you didn't know it!'

Faith's eyes grew wide as she wiggled her fingers in the air. 'Ooooh!' she sang.

I couldn't help but laugh.

Gavin clapped his hands. 'Alright then,' he said joyfully. 'We'll all meet here again before lunch tomorrow and search for Calvin. I have a feeling we're getting closer to the truth.'

Zoe and Gavin left the lunchroom holding hands *again*. Faith jogged down the hall ahead of me so she could get to her locker and make it on time to science before the bell rang.

I stood in the lobby, staring at the spot on the carpet where the kid in the hockey mask knocked me over. My vision blurred as I thought about all the problems I was having to deal with that week, which for a sixth grader, was *a lot*.

I hadn't forgotten about Wyatt stealing my ninja clan's training room. It was a bold move on his part, but an unsurprising one. He'd do anything to flip my life upside down, and he was getting really good at it. Hopefully once this talent show drama was over with, I could get to the bottom of his evil scheme.

First, Wyatt teams up with President Sebastian. Then he starts going out with Olivia Jones! There *should* be red flags all over the school, but nobody seemed to care. I could feel it in my bones – there was something going on behind the scenes, I just didn't know what it was.

My eyes followed the black skid marks from the scooters on the carpet as they curved and disappeared down the hallway. I got goosebumps. Calvin was a new kid at school, but he'd already caused enough trouble to disrupt the entire talent show.

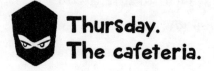 **Thursday.
The cafeteria.**

I entered the cafeteria expecting to see kids still setting up, but instead there was a crowd in front of where the stage was. I couldn't see Zoe anywhere, or *any* of my friends for that matter, so I gripped my book bag straps, kept my head down and pushed my way forward.

I couldn't see the stage, but I could see the kids who were *standing* on the stage. Red, blue and yellow lights danced on the walls, flashing on and off. Someone was messing with the strobe light at the back of the room, giving me a tiny migraine as the bright light blinked rapidly.

The speaker system had been hooked up too. A loud squeal came from the huge black boxes at the front of the room. Everyone cupped their hands over their ears, shielding themselves from the piercing sound.

The speakers thumped twice before Zoe's voice came through them. 'Check, check, one, two, checkinnnnnnng, checkinnnnnng. Can you guys hear me?'

Most of the students nodded.

'Awesome. Let's get started shall we?' she said, jumping onto the stage. I watched as she took command of the room.

'First off, I'd like to thank everyone for being here this morning and for participating in this rehearsal. You all know it was supposed to be last Monday but was rudely interrupted by some hijinks.' Zoe turned toward Sophia who was standing backstage. 'We haven't found Hotcakes yet, but we will.'

Sophia dabbed at her red nose with a ball of tissue and nodded.

Zoe went on. 'We're going to do a run-through

of everyone's acts this morning. That way we all know what to expect tomorrow.'

I made my way to the front of the room until I was next to the stage. Gavin and Faith were off to the side, watching Zoe make her announcements.

'First of all, I'm going to have everyone sit over there on the bench next to the wall in the order of when your act will perform, so the first act will take the first spot, the second act will take the second, and so on…'

The performers shuffled towards the long bench. The scaffolding with the paint cans was still directly above the bench, which was weird, but since it was just a rehearsal, I figured it would be gone by the next day.

'Howdy,' said Gavin.

'Sup,' I said. 'Any sign of Calvin?'

'Nope,' Gavin said. He pointed to the side of the room, where many of the students had already taken a seat, waiting their turn for rehearsal. 'He'll probably be over there somewhere though.'

Sophia jumped in front of us out of nowhere. 'Anything yet?' she asked, hopeful.

Gavin shook his head and stared at the floor.

'Not yet,' I said. 'But we know Hotcakes is alright. I've seen him a couple of times this week, but wasn't able to catch him.'

Sophia's eyes lit up as she cupped her hand over her mouth. 'Oh! That's good! So he's okay?'

'As far as I can tell, yeah,' I replied loudly so she could hear me over the noise in the lunchroom.

Sophia grabbed my arm. 'If you see him, you just have to yell his name! He responds to that! It's a game he likes to play! I promise he's a good penguin! He won't bite you or anything! My family has raised him since he was a little baby!'

I nodded. 'So just yell, 'Hotcakes'?'

'Yes!' she said. 'I promise you that he'll stop in place and let you to pick him up! He won't bite! I swear!'

I glanced at Gavin, but he wasn't paying

attention to Sophia. He was too busy examining the room for a kid with a patch of white hair.

When I turned back to Sophia, she was gone without a trace...until I turned to my left and saw that she had returned to her spot on the bench. Coincidentally she was seated next to Eli. They must have been the first two acts in the show because they were right up the front. The bench stretched out behind them, filled students waiting their turn. It was a little strange how they were seated because they were the only two students who *weren't* under the scaffolding.

I only noticed it because it was unlike Zoe to leave something like that unfinished. Maybe she didn't have enough people to help her get it out of the way. No big deal, I could probably get Gavin and Brayden to help me slide it backstage later.

I turned to Gavin, but before I could say anything, everyone on the bench screamed, flinching backwards. Some of the students scrambled to the floor and started running to the back of the cafeteria. The lunchroom was suddenly a mess of confusing shouts.

'It's over there! Behind the stage!'

'It looks angry! Somebody catch that thing!'

'The penguin! Someone grab that penguin! It's at the back of the room!'

I spun around, looking at the spot everyone was screaming about. They were right. The penguin was hopping back and forth, flapping its itsy-bitsy wings as it danced.

'Get it!' Zoe shouted into the microphone.

Immediately, I dashed forward. The penguin was all the way across the room, so I sprinted as hard as I could. I heard the sound of drums booming in my head as my feet hit the floor, and then I realised that someone was testing the sound system.

The penguin bolted when it saw me running at it.

He ran along the wall until it made it to the stage, then it hopped up and raced across the wooden flooring.

I kept my eye on it as it disappeared backstage again. It must've been living back there.

Mrs Olsen lifted herself onto the stage and walked carefully in case the bird jumped out. She was hunched over, staring daggers at the spot where the penguin had disappeared.

I stopped just behind Mrs Olsen and remembered what Sophia had said. Taking a deep breath, I leaned forward and shouted, 'Wait up, Hotcakes!'

Mrs Olsen spun around and glared at me. '*Excuse* me, young man? How *dare* you say such an inappropriate thing to me!'

A roar of laughter erupted from all the students behind me.

I didn't stop to explain myself. Running to the side of the stage, I climbed the stairs and made my way backstage, feeling the blood pump through my veins.

Gavin dodged Mrs Olsen and slid across the

polished surface of the stage, bouncing to his feet next to me. 'We're getting this bird today!' he shouted, running past me.

When I caught up with Gavin, he was standing just beyond the stage curtain, out of view of the cafeteria. There was a pitter-patter of tiny penguin feet. 'Where'd he go?' I asked.

'I saw him slip into that vent,' he said, pointing at the air vent behind a cardboard box. The opening was about one metre each side. He slid the box out of the way and knelt down, staring into the metal passageway.

'I don't know about this,' I said, looking at the vent.

'No, look,' Gavin said as he reached into the opening. He pushed his hand against the back wall. It fell over with a metal clang. 'This just goes through the wall. It's not an air vent at all. It's … fake.'

'What?' I asked, confused. I got down to my knees and saw what he was talking about. The air vent wasn't actually an air vent. It looked more like a hidden door or something.

'Come on,' Gavin said, crawling through the passage. 'I saw the penguin go through here.'

I nodded, questioning my ability to make smart decisions rather than dangerous and irresponsible ones. 'Alright, but let's just get Hotcakes and get out of here. I don't like the look of this.'

On the other side, Gavin and I stood up. The ceiling was so low that we had to crouch a bit in order to walk. The short hallway we were in was dark and colder than the rest of the school. It smelled musty and felt damp.

I looked at the floor expecting to see a dirt path but was surprised to see that the ground we were walking on was tiled, which meant that at some point in time, this narrow hallway was probably used quite frequently.

'You hear that?' Gavin asked.

I stopped, listening carefully. I swallowed hard as I heard the sound of a thousand thumps at the same time. Slapping noises bounced off the walls as I silently walked forward. Muffled voices shouted. Holding my breath, I stared down the hallway, realising exactly what the sound was.

There were ninjas nearby, and they were training.

'We should turn back,' Gavin said, suddenly realising the same thing.

I lifted my hand, gesturing for my friend to keep quiet. 'No way,' I said. 'This is *huge*. This *has* to be where Wyatt and the red ninjas have been training!'

'You can explore this area *later* when they're *not* here!' Gavin whispered nervously.

'I can't leave,' I said.

I was wearing my ninja outfit under my street clothes. Pulling my ninja mask over my face, I said, 'I have to see this for myself. I need to know how large his clan has grown. Just be cool and follow my lead.'

'Be cool? That's easy for you to say!' Gavin whispered harshly. 'You're wearing a mask! Where's *my* mask?'

157

I ignored Gavin's whining and walked forwards, listening as the thumping sounds of ninjas grew louder. After a few twists and turns, I found myself at the end of the passage, where there was another square opening in the wall.

I peeked out a little. What I saw was the most frightening thing I had ever seen in my life. The red ninjas were training, just as I had suspected, but their numbers were larger than I ever imagined.

The room opened up just beyond the entrance in the wall. It looked like an abandoned greenhouse or something because the ceiling was made out of glass that was caked with dirt. The sun was shining outside, but the room was dark. Book bags were set on tables against one of the walls.

Taped up to the wall was a motivational poster with a silhouette of a ninja and training times. It looked like the red ninjas trained before school *and* during lunch.

Of course! That explained why half the students were missing from the cafeteria! I also realised it meant *half* the sixth graders were

members of the red ninja clan. Wyatt was
creating an army.

'Whoa,' Gavin whispered by my side. 'This is
bad.'

'Ya think?' I said.

'Is Hotcakes in there?'

I scanned the room. 'No, I don't see him.'

'Wait a sec,' Gavin said, pushing me aside.
'Am I crazy, or is that President Sebastian?'

I looked at the front of the room. As much
as I wished it were true, Gavin *wasn't* crazy.
President Sebastian was talking to Wyatt as they
watched the red ninjas train.

'*What?*' I shouted.

The red ninjas immediately snapped their attention to the opening in the wall.

'Whoops,' I said, covering my mouth.

'Get them!' Wyatt screamed. 'Don't let them get away!'

I turned around and tried running, but tripped over Gavin's feet. We rolled across the cold floor of the secret passage.

'Get off me!' Gavin shouted.

I pulled myself up. 'Sorry about that,' I said, helping him to his feet.

Several red ninjas jumped through the opening and started sprinting at us. I pushed Gavin ahead of me. 'Where's the exit?' Gavin shouted as he ran.

'I don't know!' I said, keeping an eye on the red ninjas behind us. 'Just start turning down random corners! We'll lose these guys and find our way out when it's safe!'

'Turning down random corners doesn't sound safe!'

'Getting beat up by a bunch of ninjas is worse! Trust me!' I shouted.

Gavin darted around one of the dark corners. As I ran towards it, I kicked my foot out, hitting the wall and making a sharp right turn, following Gavin as he ran faster.

The red ninjas turned the corner easily and were quickly catching up. In the dark passageway, their red outfits seemed to glow, making them look like monsters tearing through the hall. It felt like a nightmare. Corner after corner, Gavin ran as I trailed behind him. He was probably just as scared as I was. I remembered when he had saved Zoe and me from the red ninjas the first time they chased us. I wasn't sure if we were going to find our way out of this, so I decided the least I could do was give Gavin a shot at escaping. I owed it to him.

When Gavin reached another corner, he turned left. As I made it to the same corner, I turned right. As soon as I did, I dove to the floor and rolled into the edge of the hall, where it was dark enough that it would be difficult to see me.

The red ninjas stopped at the intersection. I saw six of them total.

'Which way did Gavin go?'

'Who cares? It's Chase that we're after!'

'You three go that way, and we'll go this way.'

Three of the ninjas punched their chest and yelled, 'Ha!' And then they took off down the hall that Gavin had run down. So much for helping him escape.

The other three ninjas stepped into the passage I was in, scanning the corridor for any sign of me. They walked carefully as they approached my hiding spot.

I held my breath.

Their sneakers squeaked on the floor as they walked in front of me. I slowly exhaled, keeping as still as possible.

One of the red ninjas stopped. 'You hear that?'

His ninja buddy said, 'What?'

I could feel a bead of sweat drip down eyelid.

The red ninja pointed down the passageway. 'I heard him running! Let's go!'

When the red ninjas were far enough away,
I rolled to my feet and dusted myself off. 'Ha!'
I said. 'Suckers!'

Suddenly a thump came from behind me.
When I turned around, I saw four more red
ninjas standing in the intersection.

'Ugh!' I groaned, taking off again.

Footsteps pounded the floor behind me as
I ran harder. My side started to ache. I pressed
my hand against my ribs as I ran. If I got a
cramp at that moment, I'd be dead. My legs
were burning, and I had no idea where I was in
the school. I guess crawling through a hole in
the wall was a bad idea after all!

As hard as I tried, I couldn't do it anymore. My legs, back and sides were on fire. My gracious sprint had turned into a clumsy stumble as I slid my hand against the cold wall. I couldn't see the red ninjas in the dark passageway, but I could hear them huffing and puffing, closing in on me.

I leant against the wall and stared down the black hallway, ready to meet my enemy. Closing my eyes, I bumped my head against the wall as I caught my breath.

Suddenly, two hands grabbed my collar and pulled me off the wall. *This is it. The red ninjas have me.* But when I opened my eyes, I didn't see anyone in front of me. Instead, I saw a white figure floating above me.

'Huh?' I grunted just before getting yanked into the air. My body flew up high enough to see metal piping along the top of the passageway. I clutched at one of the pipes and pulled myself to safety.

The red ninjas sprinted past underneath me. I watched them disappear down the hall.

Catching my breath, I looked to see who my rescuer was, expecting to see an angel dressed in white robes. The truth wasn't far from that. Resting on the metal pipes next to me was another ninja, wearing white ninja robes. A full mask covered their whole face, even their eyes. From their size, I could tell they were also a sixth grader.

WHITE NINJA!?

'Who are you?' I whispered.

The white ninja stared at me for a second, silently. And then shrugged and dropped to the floor.

I landed on the ground next to him, keeping an eye out for any other red ninjas. Taking a few steps down the passageway, I said, 'Thanks for saving my butt back there. I would've been dead meat if it hadn't been for—'

When I turned around, the white ninja was gone.

The butterflies in my stomach started flying again. On top of all the other junk I had to deal with, now I had to add a *white ninja* to the list? Were they friend or foe? Wyatt was supposed to be a friend when I first met him, but we all know how *that* turned out.

After a few minutes, I found another way out of the passageway. There was an opening that led to the library. I didn't doubt that the secret passage was how Wyatt and his red ninjas moved around the school so quickly. If there was an entrance backstage in the cafeteria and in the library, there were sure to be more.

I pulled my ninja mask off just as the bell rang. School was starting and I had no idea where Gavin had gone. For all I knew, he had been captured by Wyatt and was being held prisoner in that secret room. The thought made my head spin.

**Thursday.
Gym class.**

I went back to the cafeteria to look for
Gavin after first period, but he wasn't there.
Zoe asked if we had caught the penguin. I was
sad to tell her no. When she asked where Gavin
was, I was sadder to tell her I didn't know.

I waited in the hallway until the last possible
second to see if Gavin would appear, but he
never did. Unsure of what to do, I went to
class. I hoped things would turn out alright,
but I seriously doubted it.

On the football field, I stood on the sidelines,
wearing the dumb moose outfit again. The

other students fell in line behind their teams so they could get the game started.

Jake stepped onto the field, but he didn't approach his team. Instead, he walked towards me. His wolf pack followed obediently behind him, their red wristbands flopping on their arms.

When he was a metre away from me, he stopped, folded his arms, and stared into my eyes. 'Why even bother wearing the mask anymore?' he asked.

'Uh, because I'm not on a team, so coach is making me wear it,' I replied.

'No,' Jake said, shaking his head. 'I mean your *ninja* mask. Why bother wearing it if we all know who you are already?'

I sat there for a moment. 'Because not everyone knows who I am.'

'The kids who matter do,' a voice said from behind me.

It was Wyatt. He had found his way to the football field. I looked past him, trying to see if Coach Cooper was outside. He was in his usual spot, reclining in a lawn chair and sipping on lemonade.

As hall monitor captain, Wyatt had a few extra privileges, such as walking the halls whenever he wanted to make sure everyone was in class. Needless to say he was taking advantage of that privilege.

'We have your friend, you know,' Wyatt said. '*Gavin*.'

'Where is he?' I asked, upset.

Wyatt tugged on his shirtsleeves, refolding them as he said, 'In a safe place ... for now.'

'You can't hold kids prisoner,' I said. 'That's not just frowned upon – I'm pretty sure that's illegal.'

Wyatt smiled softly. 'I guess the ball's in my court now,' he paused, looking at the two football teams on the field. 'I mean, in my *possession* now.'

I said nothing.

'So how's this sound,' Wyatt said. 'You have to do whatever I say or I'll tell Principal Davis *everything* about you.'

It felt like the wind had just been knocked out of me.

Wyatt grinned. 'I'll give you a moment to think about it.'

A couple of months ago, Wyatt had stolen my ninja outfit from my book bag. He pulled a series of random crimes while wearing the robes and made sure to get a photo taken of each one. It didn't take long for the school paper to get wind of the story and from there, a ninja in black robes became one of the most wanted students the school had ever seen. They never caught Wyatt while he was in my outfit, but hall monitors were still searching for the mysterious ninja.

So you could see how Wyatt telling Principal Davis about my ninja clan wouldn't be the most awesome thing ever... *I* would be the one who got busted for those crimes.

I stared at Wyatt. I had no doubt that he'd tell Principal Davis about my secret ninja clan. Even though I was framed, I wasn't sure anyone would want to hear my side of the story.

Wyatt chomped on his spearmint gum like a dimwitted camel. The sloshing sound was unnerving. There he was – the worst bully I'd ever stood before, threatening to tell on me.

I shook my head. There was no way I was gonna go down like that. He had power and he was trying to hold it over my head like a balloon filled with water. If I upset him, he'd pop the balloon and soak me to my skin.

But then a crazy thing happened in my head. I blinked a couple of times, collecting my thoughts, and suddenly everything became clear to me.

All I had to do was take that power away from him.

I chuckled as the realisation hit me. He said he'd give me a moment to think about it, but all I needed was a millisecond.

I pulled the moose mask off and dropped it to the ground with a thud. Most of the gym class gasped when they realised it was me in the costume, but I didn't really care. Spinning

around, I began marching across the field, back
to the school.

'Wait,' Wyatt muttered. 'What're you doing?
Where are you going?'

'I'm going to tell Principal Davis *myself*,' I
shouted.

I could hear Wyatt's panic as he spoke to
Jake and his crew. 'Is he serious? He's going to
go to the principal? That's madness! What's
wrong with him?'

My smile stretched wider across my face.

Wyatt's footsteps beat against the grassy field
as he caught up to me. Cutting me off, he held

his hands up. 'Fine, dude! You win! We don't have Gavin! Just don't go to Davis and tell him everything, okay?'

I stopped walking. 'What do you mean you *don't* have Gavin?'

Wyatt caught his breath, reluctant to tell me the truth. Finally, he squeezed his eyes shut and gave up. 'My ninjas couldn't find him after you two split up. He got away from us, alright? I was *lying* to you to get you to do what I wanted. You called my bluff. Happy? Gavin's in class right now – fit as a fiddle, snug as a bug, cosy as a cat! However you wanna say it! He's fine!'

I looked Wyatt in the eye. He looked more worried than angry. 'How do you know he's in class?' I asked.

Wyatt put his hands on his hips and glared at me. 'I'm the hall monitor captain, remember? I checked on him after the bell rang. He didn't even look fazed.'

For about two seconds, I forgot that Wyatt was the bad guy. Then it all came back to me.

I stepped forward, tapping my finger against his chest. 'Principal Davis has no clue about you or your ninjas, does he?'

'Of course he doesn't!' Wyatt said sternly. 'Are you nuts?'

I stepped past the leader of the red ninja clan and continued towards the locker rooms. Gym wasn't over, but I'd already had all the exercise I could handle for that day. Coach Cooper wouldn't let me out of class until it was over, but I knew he wouldn't mind if I took it easy right next to him. Maybe he had an extra glass of lemonade.

'Chase!' Wyatt shouted.

I spun around, waiting for him to speak.

'We're ninjas,' he said. 'And we live by a code, you and I. It's like the bro code, but with ninjas.'

'And what's that?' I asked. 'I thought the bro code meant you couldn't date your friend's ex-girlfriend or something.'

'Okay, it's nothing like the bro code then,' Wyatt admitted. 'The point is that I'd never tell anyone about your secret identity, and I hope you'd do the same for me. I bluffed when I said I'd tell Principal Davis, but you should know it was an empty threat.'

I was confused. 'Why are you telling me this?'

'Because I feel like I owe it to you,' Wyatt explained. 'That's at least one thing you can be sure about of me.'

Wyatt turned around and hiked back to the football field. I chewed my lip, confused. Since the beginning of the school year, Wyatt had been nothing but trouble for me. Was it possible that maybe he was starting to let up a little? From my experience with him, the answer should've been no, but everyone deserves a second chance...

Don't they?

**Thursday.
Lunch.**

When I got to the cafeteria, I still couldn't find
Gavin. Several kids from my ninja clan were
already in the cafeteria wearing their normal
street clothes. I nodded to them as I walked
through the doors, feeling a bit sheepish at
having lost our base for a *second* time since
becoming their leader. I wish I could tell them
I had a plan to fix everything, but the truth
was that I didn't. I felt exhausted and stretched
thin after everything that had happened this
week, like a drop of syrup trying to cover a
stack of pancakes.

After a minute of walking aimlessly, I saw Gavin sitting with Zoe and Faith. I was happy to see he wasn't a prisoner somewhere in the dungeon of the school. I dragged my feet across the ground towards them.

'You look tired,' Faith said when she noticed me.

'I am,' I replied, taking a seat next to her.

'Well, you can take it easy,' Zoe said. 'We haven't been able to find Calvin anywhere in here.'

I looked around the cafeteria. I wasn't surprised to see that a lot of the other sixth graders were missing. It wasn't like it was totally empty, but it was at least empty enough that even a few of the teachers standing against the wall had started to notice.

'You know where he probably is?' I asked, feeling a pit in my stomach at the thought of the red ninjas secret greenhouse training room.

Gavin nodded, but didn't say anything. I didn't either because I didn't want to freak out Zoe or Faith.

'Where?' Zoe asked. 'In fact, it seems like a bunch of kids have been absent this week, hasn't it?'

Faith shrugged a shoulder. 'Just during lunch,' she said. 'All my classes have been full, which is weird because the cafeteria seems so empty.'

I kept quiet, fully knowing that the missing kids were training as red ninjas.

Zoe turned around, trying to peer through the tinted glass walls of the cafeteria so she could see the library, which was directly on the other side of the hall. 'They better not be in the library! I'd *hate* if that room got flooded with a bunch of students. I'd *never* find a seat.'

'Doubt it,' Faith joked. 'Maybe the cafeteria is just getting bigger?'

I stood up. 'I'm gonna take a look around,' I said sombrely as I started to walk away from the table.

Gavin started to get up, but I raised my hand. 'It's cool,' I said. 'I just want to be alone for now.'

Dropping back into his chair, Gavin faced Zoe and Faith again. I could hear their jokes as

I walked farther down the aisle. I hoped their feelings weren't hurt. I just needed to be in my own head.

All of the talent show gear was set up, waiting for Friday, which was less than twenty-four hours away. I had an awful feeling that Calvin was going to pull some prank during the show, wrecking it for everyone. It was so weird trying to picture it all happening because in my mind, Calvin's face was blank since I didn't know who he was or what he even looked like.

I knew that if I wanted to find Calvin, I could start with the greenhouse. The only thing about that was that it'd be *filled* with members of the red ninja clan, and I probably wouldn't make it out without at least one black eye as a souvenir.

'Mr Chase Cooper!' said a boy's voice from behind me.

I spun around, looking at the kid who said my name. I was a bit taken back when I recognised him. 'President Sebastian?'

PRESIDENT
SEBASTIAN

Sebastian held his open hand out to me. He was dressed in a fancy light grey suit with a red striped necktie. Standing behind him were two other boys in suits, both wearing aviator sunglasses and occasionally tossing a glance over their shoulders. 'Pleased to finally meet you,' the president said.

I took his hand, gripped it tightly, and shook it like I was in a business meeting. 'Likewise,' I said.

Grasping my hand firmly, the president yanked me close enough so he could whisper,

'I *know* you were in the greenhouse yesterday. I know it was *you*.'

I pulled my hand away. 'So what?' I said, frustrated and angry that Sebastian wasn't there to make peace. 'I'm sure Wyatt filled you in on *all* the details, didn't he?'

Sebastian tugged at his coat sleeve. 'No,' he said. 'Wyatt never said a word about you. It was his cousin, Carlyle.'

'What's Carlyle got to do with it?' I asked, and then I realised I actually had no clue what was happening at all. 'No, wait. Start way back from the beginning. What's your deal with Wyatt? Why'd you give him the position of hall monitor captain?'

'Doesn't Wyatt deserve it?' Sebastian asked softly.

I was so shocked that I had to lift my jaw off the floor. 'No,' I said firmly. 'He *doesn't* deserve it! You're planning something, and I know it.'

'Oh, do you?' Sebastian asked, folding his arms.

'Well, no,' I said, 'but I assume that you are…
since everything you've done so far has been
shady.'

'Welcome to the real world,' Sebastian
laughed. His face suddenly tightened. He glared
at me and said, 'Not that you can do anything
to stop us now, but you best mind your
business, *son*. Or else you're *done*. 'Cause we've
already *won*.'

I just about cracked up because he sounded
like a kids' rhyming book. 'Yeah? Was it *fun*?
When you *won* under the *sun* tanning yo' *buns*?'

Sebastian's face flushed with anger. He
pointed at me. 'Just stay out of our way, or
you'll be sorry!'

The two hall monitors stepped aside,
allowing President Sebastian to walk through
them. I watched as they used the kitchen doors
to exit the cafeteria instead of the doors at the
front of the room.

I knew that kid was up to something before,
but now I *really* knew it. Unfortunately, I didn't
know what he was scheming. I doubted that it

had anything to do with the talent show since Sebastian's shady actions had started long before Zoe had even talked about putting it on.

Staring at the back of the stage, I thought about the white ninja that had saved me from getting my butt handed to me in a doggy bag. Was he a good guy or a bad guy? Since he helped me get away, I could only hope he was on my side.

**Friday.
The talent show.**

Finally, the day of the talent show had arrived and everyone was in high spirits. Zoe was running around like a superhero, supervising every little detail.

Students were lined up on the stage, reading sheets of paper that probably had the schedule for the morning. The stage that Gavin had fixed looked awesome and solid as a rock. In fact, if I didn't know the corner was busted earlier in the week, I'd never have been able to tell.

Overnight, a crew had set up fold-out chairs in rows for the audience. The cafeteria lights had been switched off and the talent show stage lights were being tested, making the room look like some sort of dance club.

The only students in the cafeteria were those who had acts in the show. Everyone was standing around, laughing and having a good time. I was relieved see others enjoying themselves. The missing penguin had been in everyone's thoughts all week, but nobody knew that Hotcakes might've been just the tip of the iceberg.

The rest of the sixth graders would arrive in about twenty minutes when homeroom was dismissed. The first half of the school day was dedicated to Zoe's talent show, which was killer because it meant all those classes would be put on hold, but it also meant the last half of the day's classes would be put on hold too, replaced with a three-hour outdoor lunch. The entire day was basically a free day.

Gavin was sitting on the edge of the stage so I had to weave between students to get to him. Just beyond the stage curtain were props for different acts.

Some bright blue frisbees caught my eye
right away. They were extra cool because they
had a four-pointed star printed on them that
reminded me of ninja stars.

I heard Zoe's voice nearby. 'I don't
understand why that scaffolding is here still,'
she growled. 'It's such an eyesore!'

Looking to my left, I saw her venting some
frustration to Gavin and Faith.

'When people look back on this day, all
they're gonna think of is that ugly scaffolding!'

Zoe said, pointing at it. 'Look! Someone even left paint cans on top of it!'

Gavin patted the air. I think it's becoming his signature move. 'Relax,' he said calmly. 'I'll find Adam and figure it all out. You just worry about the talent show.'

Zoe held up her clipboard. 'I'm sorry,' she said. 'There's just so much to do before the show starts, which is in about twenty minutes.' She looked over at me. 'Oh, good! You're here! Could you do me a favour?'

'Of course,' I said.

Zoe pointed to a couple of fold-out chairs leaning against the front of the stage. 'Could you take those backstage? We've got enough chairs out here.'

I wrapped my hands around the two chairs, surprised by how heavy they were. I played it off like it was no big deal. Smiling a little too wide, I struggled to say, 'No problemo!'

Zoe returned to her clipboard and walked to the back of the cafeteria. Gavin and Faith followed, waiting for instructions.

I took the chairs backstage and leaned them against the wall. Opening and closing my fists, I tried to squeeze the pain out of them, hissing through my teeth.

And that's when I saw him. *Hotcakes.* He was poking his head out from the small opening in the wall.

'Seriously?' I said. As I slowly approached, I spoke softly. 'There's no way I'm gonna scream your name while I'm back here so please just let me grab your tiny little bird body...'

Hotcakes stared at my outstretched hands. He jerked his body, shivering, but didn't move.

'Goooooood birdie,' I sang. 'Goooooooood biiiiiiiiirdie.'

Hotcakes hopped forward and hissed at me.

I flinched, reeling my hands back in, and scolded the penguin through my clenched teeth. 'You're being a bad penguin! You know that? *Bad* penguin!'

Instead of running back into the opening in the wall, Hotcakes darted further backstage, zooming like a tiny missile.

I considered calling out for help, but decided against it. It was still early in the morning so the red ninjas were sure to be training in the greenhouse. I couldn't risk them hearing me.

I followed Hotcakes backstage. 'Heeeeeeere, Hotcaaaaaaakes,' I whispered. 'Heeeeeeere, frustrating little bird that has wings but can't fly.'

The cardboard boxes along the walls shook slightly, one after the other. Reminding myself that Sophia said Hotcakes was perfectly safe and wouldn't bite, I continued to follow him through the cramped path backstage.

I kept my distance as Hotcakes bumped into different boxes and hanging costumes. Every few seconds, the penguin would dash across the narrow corridor, disturbing all the junk on the other side. If I didn't know it was a penguin, I would've been freaked out that I had just found a ghost.

Soon the hallway narrowed so much that it was impossible to keep going. The short stack of cardboards boxes against the end of the corridor jostled and then suddenly stopped.

'What?' I said, confused. Slowly moving my foot forward, I slid the short stack of cardboard boxes out of the way.

On the other side of the boxes, where I thought the backstage ended, was a thin metal door that was pushed open about fifteen centimetres. The penguin must've gone into the next room.

I opened the door all the way and found a set of stairs. It was only half a flight, and I wasn't surprised to see Hotcakes at the top, peeking out at me almost mockingly.

Steadily, I walked up the stairs without taking my eyes off the penguin. But as the rest of the room came into view, I almost forgot he was even there.

You know that point in a movie when the hero suddenly makes a life-changing discovery? Like, the camera shows them walking over a small, rocky hill as a massive background reveals itself, and the orchestra music starts slowly swelling until the camera swings around and shows you the shocked look on the hero's face. That's when the drums start pounding in the background, and it's almost like the hero has been transformed…

Yeah, *that's* how it felt as I walked up those dirty steps.

At the top of the staircase, the room completely opened up. It was so large that I felt tiny standing in the middle of it. My sneakers squished on the ground with each step I took. When I looked down, I saw that I was walking on wrestling mats that covered the entire floor.

The walls were concrete blocks with flags hanging from them. Each flag represented a year that Buchanan had won a wrestling tournament. The last flag at the far end of the room had '1999' on it.

If the red ninjas weren't training here, they didn't know it even existed. Ideas started racing through my mind of how awesome it would be if my ninja clan had a place like this to train in.

I heard a chirp at my feet. When I looked down, Hotcakes was nestled against my calf. A small part of me couldn't shake the idea that maybe Hotcakes had brought me here on purpose. Carefully, I reached down and wrapped my hands around him. He didn't try to wriggle free.

A door across the room creaked open. Coach

Cooper stepped through and walked over to the light switch on the wall. He stopped when he noticed me. 'Chase?' he asked. 'What're you doing—' he paused, pointing at the bird in my hands. 'You found the penguin!'

'I did!' I laughed.

'Did you follow it in here?' Coach Cooper asked.

'Yeah,' I said. 'It came in through the door down the steps.'

Coach Cooper nodded. 'Nice work, kiddo. Sophia will be glad to hear it, but probably not as much as Principal Davis.' The coach continued to the light switch on the wall and flipped the lights off. He gestured to the stairs I had walked up. 'Go back that way and shut the door, would ya?'

I started to turn around, but paused, remembering my ninja clan was without a home. 'Hey, coach?' I said.

Coach Cooper turned around in the doorway. 'Yeah?'

'What's the deal with this room?'

Leaning against the doorframe, Coach Cooper spoke softly. 'Back in the day, we used to have a wrestling team, but the program was cut due to funding. This room is all that's left.'

'So it's not being used for anything?' I asked, hugging the penguin in my arms.

The coach sighed. 'Sometimes it's used for gymnastics week, but for the rest of the year, it's locked up.'

'Is it something I could use?' I asked immediately. 'I mean, if I started some kind of athletics club or something?'

'Don't see why not,' the coach said, scanning the room. 'It's empty like this all the time. The only condition is that the wrestling mats have to be cleaned daily.'

That was a small price to pay for a full-size training arena. 'No problem,' I said, smiling.

The coach pointed at the stairs behind me again. 'What kind of *athletics* club do you want to start?'

I paused, trying to think of a good answer. I didn't want to say I was going to use it for ninja training, but I also didn't want to lie. 'Martial arts,' I said finally.

'Cool,' Coach Cooper said, giving me a thumbs up. 'Get back out to the talent show, Chase. We can discuss details afterwards.'

I didn't hesitate. I jumped down the steps, clearing all of them in one leap. Hotcakes didn't seem to mind.

After leaving the secret wrestling room, I pushed the short stack of boxes back against the thin metal door. I didn't want to risk Wyatt or any members of his ninja clan finding it.

The noise from the kids preparing for the talent show flooded the backstage area. As I marched down the narrow corridor, I found the cage that Hotcakes had escaped from. Gently, I set him back into it, and shut the metal gate, locking the latch.

'Sorry, Hotcakes,' I said, 'but I think it's best if I keep you in here while I find Sophia.'

The penguin chirped at me.

Jogging back to the cafeteria, I hopped from backstage onto the lunchroom floor. Zoe was still running back and forth between her crew, barking orders. Along the wall, I saw most of the students in the talent show sitting on the bench, waiting their turn. Eli and Sophia were the first two students on the bench.

I was just about to shout for Sophia when someone grabbed my shirt collar with two hands and pulled me aside. It was Adam. Gavin was standing right behind him.

'What're you doing?' I asked.

Adam's eyes were wide as he spoke frantically. 'I saw *Calvin* outside in the lobby!' he said. 'I overheard him say something about messing with the stage again!'

Gavin stepped closer. 'We gotta find him before he does anything!'

'We should go to Principal Davis about this, shouldn't we?' I suggested.

'There's no time!' Adam said. 'You have to go out there and stop him!'

'But we don't even know what this kid looks like!' I said, feeling a little panicked.

'He's wearing an orange shirt with stripes!' Adam said, pushing me toward the cafeteria doors.

'Alright, fine!' I said. 'Just let go of me!'

Gavin pulled open the door and left first. I followed, pressing the fabric of my collar down, trying to undo the damage Adam had done. There were tiny pink and green threads all over my shirt – probably from when Adam had grabbed me. It was annoying having to wipe them all off. I knew I had seen that kind of thread before, but I couldn't remember where.

I was so distracted trying to fix my shirt that I didn't even notice Wyatt trying to enter the room. I stepped forward, accidentally knocking into him. He fell into the cafeteria door and bounced to the ground. A cup of water spilled down the front of his outfit.

'*Really?*' Wyatt shouted, angry.

I stepped over him and chuckled. 'Sorry, man!' I said, and honestly. 'Seriously, I didn't mean to do that!'

'You soaked my shirt!' Wyatt shouted. 'Where are you going? Get *back* here!'

I slipped into the crowd of students, following Gavin. If I had stayed to let Wyatt yell at me, I know the situation would've just got worse. Even though I didn't want to, I knew I'd find him later to apologise because it actually *was* my fault.

The lobby of the school was so full of sixth graders that it was almost impossible to move. As Gavin pushed through the crowd, I did my best to stay as close to him as possible.

'You see him?' Gavin asked over the noisy crowd.

'A kid with an orange shirt?' I asked. 'Nope.'

Gavin zigzagged through the students, checking each t-shirt. Then he stopped, and shouted, 'Calvin? Does anyone know a Calvin?'

The crowd of students ignored the question, except for the few girls nearby that shot dirty looks at Gavin for yelling in their ears.

I clutched the back of Gavin's shirt so I wouldn't lose him. 'There's no way we're gonna find him in all this,' I said. 'This is hopeless!'

'We can't just give up,' Gavin replied.

'What if we stood by the doors and checked everyone's shirt as they entered the cafeteria?' I suggested.

'We need to find him *before* he gets in there,' Gavin said. 'We can't risk him sabotaging the stage—'

Abruptly, Gavin stopped talking and darted forward, grabbing another student's elbow.

When he pulled the student closer, I saw the orange shirt with stripes. It had to be the kid Adam talked about! It *had* to be Calvin!

Gavin's face twisted angrily. 'It's over, Calvin! We *know* what you're planning!'

The boy in Gavin's grip looked confused. 'What? What're you talking about? Who's Calvin?'

'*You* are,' I said after a pause.

The boy escaped Gavin's grip. 'No, I'm not! My name is Max.'

Principal Davis suddenly appeared next to us, as if he'd teleported to that spot. 'What's the problem here? Gavin? Chase? What're you two doing?'

Gavin spoke quickly, trying to defend himself. 'We were trying to stop Calvin from—'

'Calvin?' the principal asked, confused.

'Yeah,' I said, pointing at the kid in the orange shirt. 'His name is Calvin...we think.'

'No,' Principal Davis said, shaking his head. 'This boy's name is Max.'

Max folded his arms and stared daggers at me.

And then the principal said something that totally blew my mind. 'There's nobody at this school named Calvin. Trust me, I would know – that's my name too.'

My jaw just about hit the floor. That couldn't be possible, could it? We had spent the entire week searching for someone named Calvin. Sophia, Eli *and* Adam said they saw Calvin messing with the penguin cage and the stage. But now Principal Davis was telling us he didn't exist?

I felt an itch on the front of my neck from where Adam had left all those tiny pink and green threads. When I scratched it, I suddenly remembered where I had seen those threads. It was the same pink and green thread that was on the rope tied to the scaffolding. The same scaffolding that had paint cans nailed to the top of it. The same scaffolding that was still in the lunchroom, looming over the heads of all the talent show acts.

All the acts *except* for Sophia and Eli.

My eye twitched. There was so many dots connecting in my mind that I was scared my head would burst.

I spun around and ran back to the cafeteria windows. Cupping my hands on the tinted glass, I squinted so I could see clearly.

Adam was messing around backstage. He was alone, and I could see that the braided rope was in his hands He had the rope wound around his fists and he was pulling gently at it.

I followed the rope with my eyes. It was partially hidden by the stage curtain that hung in front of it. On the other side of the curtain, along the cafeteria floor, the rope trailed all the way back to the bench along the wall, where it curved upward and was tied to the wooden plank on top of the scaffolding, which *still* hadn't been removed from the cafeteria.

On top of the plank, I saw the paint cans that had been nailed into place, but there were more cans up there now and the lids had been popped open.

Every student in the talent show had taken their place on the bench. The students were all seated *under* the scaffolding, except for Sophia and Eli, who were just on the other side of the metal cage, safe from the paint cans above.

My mouth felt dry as I realised that one good tug from Adam and the plank with the paint cans would flip over, dumping paint all over the kids in the talent show. *Except* for Sophia and Eli.

'Good gravy,' I whispered.

Those three had been playing us all week!

I pushed my way through the crowd and jumped back into the cafeteria. I wasn't sure if Gavin was behind me or not, but I couldn't waste any time to check.

Glancing at the clock, I saw that there were still a few minutes until the talent show officially started. Zoe was back at the sounding-board, making final adjustments to the speaker system. Gavin was still in the lobby,

PAINT CANS

SCAFFOLD

ROPE

UNSUSPECTING STUDENTS!

SOPHIA

ELI

Faith was nowhere to be seen, and neither was Brayden.

Sneaking along the wall, I climbed the steps to the backstage and scanned the area. Adam was hidden behind the curtain on the opposite side of the stage, holding the braided rope in his hands. When was he going to pull it?

'Places everyone!' Zoe said over the speakers. 'The show starts...*now*!'

I stared at Adam from across the stage as the sixth graders poured into the cafeteria.

Conversation and laughter filled the air as kids took their seats in the audience. If I ran across the stage, someone would definitely notice me. I didn't want Adam to freak out and pull the rope, so I waited, thinking of what my next move should be.

And then something hit me in the back, knocking me to the floor. The stage curtain had been pushed to the side, blocking anyone from seeing me.

'Our leader thinks you oughta be punished!' said a raspy voice.

When I rolled over, I saw five red ninjas standing over me. Wonderful, I thought. This day just getting worse and worse.

'How 'bout we do this another time?' I said, standing up. 'Wyatt can play bully all he wants on Monday, I promise, as long as you guys leave me alone right now.'

The red ninja in front shot his foot out at me. Obviously they weren't going to listen. I tried dodging the attack, but it struck me right in the chest. The force from the kick knocked me backwards. As I stumbled over my feet, I knew I was going to land out in the open in front of everyone. I pulled my ninja mask over my head.

I was finally able to stop myself in the middle of the stage, in front of every sixth grader in the school. I stood up slowly. Everyone was staring at me. Hushed whispers filtered through the room about the ninja on stage.

I thought for sure the red ninjas would keep themselves hidden, but they boldly stepped out into the open and formed a circle around me. I couldn't believe what was happening. Were these guys really looking for a fight? On a stage? In front of the entire grade?

One of the red ninjas balled his fists and pointed them at me. 'Sup, *nerdling*,' he said from behind his mask.

I studied the ninja's eyes. 'Jake,' I whispered.

'You embarrassed me on the field,' Jake said. 'Now it's time for a little payback.'

The other four red ninjas slowly started circling me. My heart raced as I looked out into the room. Principal Davis was standing at the back just *watching*! *Why wasn't anyone trying to stop this?*

I scanned the room until I made eye contact with Zoe. She was back by the sounding-board, glaring at me with her arms crossed. I had no doubt she knew it was me on the stage, dressed in a black ninja outfit.

Jake turned, punched his fist into his open palm, and bowed to the crowd. Everyone clapped, and then I realised that was why nobody was doing anything – they thought it was part of the show!

I sunk down on one foot and raised my open hands, taking a defensive stance. I stared at the open space in front of me, allowing my eyes to relax so I could see everything by looking at nothing.

I've said it a million times before, but I'm against fighting. I won't throw a punch even if one is thrown at me. Faith helped me realise that a couple of months ago at the skating party. The second I throw a punch, I just become another kid who got in a fight at school. Standing up to bullies meant that I couldn't bring myself down to their level – and *fighting* a stupid fight would've done just that. I'm Chase Cooper, and I *knew* I was better than that.

Orange spotlights started pulsing on and off. Apparently the kid by the light board thought he'd try and make things look cooler. I'm sure to the audience it did, but it was a little distracting for me.

The tallest of the red ninjas threw a couple of intimidation lunges at me, saying, '*What? You want some? What now, huh? What?*'

I had to look up because the ninja was so tall. They must've been the same height as an adult, but there was no way any *teachers* were in Wyatt's red ninja clan. And then I remembered that there *was* one student that was, like, two metres tall. It was probably her.

Jake jumped at me first, spinning in the air and launching a kick at my head. I trusted that my reflexes would respond because I knew if I thought about it too hard, I'd freeze up and get pummelled. It worked perfectly.

I casually stepped to the side, and Jake sailed straight past me. Two of the red ninjas in front came at me at the same time, throwing fists in the air like they just didn't care. I put my hands

behind my back and leaned to the side, dodging both punches like it was my job.

'Thanks for the offer, but I think I'll pass on your punches today,' I added sarcastically.

Spinning around, I faced all five red ninjas. I kept my hands behind my back. Honestly, I felt like some sort of wise old ninja guru playing with a bunch of kids. I had to smile.

Jake ran forward, screaming some sort of battle cry. I shifted my feet so my body twisted sideways, blocking his punch with my elbow. Frustrated, Jake tossed out a flurry of jabs.

I leaned away from most of the attacks. The rest I continued to block with my elbow. The craziest part about it was the way time slowed down as it happened. After each attack, I watched as he slowly dragged his arm through space, giving me enough time to just step away.

The sixth graders in the crowd cheered each time I dodged an attack. They had no idea it was an actual fight, but they probably wouldn't have cared since nobody was actually landing any hits.

Several of the red ninjas ran towards me at the same time, a few taking the high road, while the rest took the low. I leaned over and spun on my feet, letting the ninjas kick at the air above me. When they were past, I continued my spin, raising one of my knees to avoid a low spinning sweep at my legs.

I was feeling good, better than I ever had in my life, but that came to an end pretty quickly. When I turned to face the ninjas, Jake was diving towards me. I tried to move out of the way, but it was too late.

Jake's shoulder smashed into me, knocking me to the ground. The audience gasped, probably shocked because the attack looked and sounded so real. They didn't know it *was* real.

Tasting blood in my mouth, I set my knee on the ground and looked up just in time to see Jake coming in for his finishing move. Lifting my arms, I blocked my face, but instead of feeling pain, I felt a rush of air blast past me, and then a loud *whoomph*.

I heard Jake's muffled shouts. When I opened my eyes, Jake wasn't standing in front of me. Instead, I was staring at the mysterious white ninja. He was standing like a superhero on top of a small mountain of red velvet that looked like a curtain. And then I realised it *was* the curtain.

The white ninja had dropped the stage curtain on the red ninjas in order to save me! The white ninja *was* on my side!

'Who are you?' I asked.

The white ninja turned toward me, his mask fully covering his entire face.

'A friend,' he said in a low growl, obviously disguising his voice.

Spinning in a circle, the white ninja threw a small pouch at the floor. It popped, instantly creating a white cloud of chalk dust. When the dust cleared, the white ninja was gone.

'*Awesome!*' I whispered.

The audience burst into applause, thinking it was part of the act. Everyone stood up, shouting loudly, completely clueless about what had actually happened.

I scooted to the back of the stage and took my ninja mask off. The red ninjas were still struggling under the red velvet curtain.

I glanced across the room and saw Adam. His mouth was wide open as he stared at the curtain too, but his hand was still gripping the rope attached to the scaffolding.

I stepped forward, accidentally catching his attention. His eyebrows furrowed as his eyes flashed with rage. Grasping the rope with both hands, he yanked it to the side, pulling it hard.

My eyes darted to scaffolding. The plank of wood, along with the paint cans, started tipping over.

Frantically, I searched the stage for anything that could help me, and saw the frisbees. I dove across the stage and grabbed one. Spinning my arm out wide, I flung the frisbee as hard as I could at the spot above the contestants.

The crowd was still busy cheering for the ninja performance that they didn't notice what was happening. I watched with wide eyes as the frisbee flew across the room. The plank tipped further and further until finally…

CRANK!

The frisbee lodged itself between the plank and the scaffolding, jamming tightly in place. The four-pointed star stuck out like a ninja star. The paint cans spilled a couple of drops of paint over their rims, but nothing fell from the scaffolding. 'Ha!' I shouted, raising a fist into the air.

Adam dropped the rope and ran down the side of the stage. He jumped to the floor and headed towards one the side exit of the cafeteria. He kicked the door open and ran out. Sophia and Eli bolted from their place on the bench and ran out the door too.

Gavin sprinted across the back of the room, jumping over empty metal chairs. I know Zoe would have followed him, but she still had to run the talent show. I leapt off the stage and joined Gavin at the side exit where Adam, Sophia and Eli had escaped. Without saying a word, Gavin pushed the door open and together we stepped through.

On the other side of the door, I was expecting another chase through the halls. Needless to say, I was pleasantly surprised.

215

Adam, Sophia and Eli were in the middle of an argument in the empty hallway.

'*My* fault?' Sophia shouted. '*You* were the one who said Hotcakes wouldn't be out of his cage for more than a minute! He's been missing all week!'

'The plan was *working*!' Adam shouted defensively. 'If you had just stuck to the original plan, we would've got away with *all* of this!'

Principal Davis and Coach Cooper stepped through the cafeteria doors and into the hall. The principal folded his arms and shook his head.

Adam pointed down the hallway and

suddenly had a frightened look upon his face. 'There! The kid who set Sophia's penguin loose ran that way! If you hurry, you can catch him!'

Sophia's face grew bright red, and if she were a cartoon character, I'm sure steam would've shot out of her ears.

'That's enough!' she shouted. 'I've had *enough* of this lying and cheating!'

Adam waved his hands around and opened his eyes wide at Sophia. 'You're just frustrated, that's all! You've lost your penguin and are just having an *angry* moment, okay? We should all just calm down and count to—'

'No!' Sophia said. 'I'm *done* with this! I played along all week, but I'm *done* now! *None* of this is worth it!'

Principal Davis spoke sternly. '*Someone* tell me what this is all about.'

'This is about Adam cheating so we could win the talent show!' Sophia said.

Adam began stumbling over his words as he tried to defend himself.

Sophia spoke louder so Adam couldn't.

'Adam's been planning on dumping paint all over the other kids in the talent show!'

'I *knew* it!' I shouted.

Everyone looked at me.

I kicked the floor, embarrassed.

Sophia continued. 'Adam rigged the scaffolding above everyone so that he could yank a rope to tip the wooden plank over on top. The paint cans were nailed to the wood so that the cans themselves wouldn't fall off and hurt anyone.'

'Come on!' Adam said. 'That doesn't even sound like something a kid would do! I mean, really? Scheme a diabolical plan? Bah!'

'You *did* it and you *know* it!' Sophia said, angry. 'After the paint dropped on everyone, there would only be two students left in the talent show – Eli and me. Since we would be the last two contestants, it didn't matter which one of us won because we'd all split the thousand-dollar prize three ways. Three hundred and thirty bucks each, with the leftover ten dollars for ice cream cones to celebrate.'

'So the penguin was your part, and Adam was supposed to pull the rope,' Principal Davis said, 'but what about Eli? What's his role in all this?'

Sophia pressed her lips together. 'It was Eli's job to set Hotcakes free on Monday, which he did.'

'*You* were the kid in the hockey mask?' Gavin asked Eli.

Eli caved. 'Yes,' he whispered. 'My job was to open the cage and run, creating a diversion so Adam could pull the rope. Everyone was supposed to get splashed with orange paint during Monday morning's rehearsal.'

'So what happened?' Gavin asked.

'Well, the rope didn't work on Monday,' Eli said. 'It wasn't tied tight enough.'

'And the broken stage?' Gavin said.

'That was an accident,' Eli admitted. 'I banged into it as I was racing out of the room.'

'Why didn't Sophia just set her own penguin free?' Gavin asked.

Sophia spoke again. 'Adam said it would be

less obvious if someone *other* than the penguin's owner set it free. That way I'd still be in the cafeteria worried sick about Hotcakes.'

'Wait, wait, wait,' Gavin said, holding his palms up. 'So who's Calvin?'

'Calvin doesn't exist!' Sophia said. 'If anyone suspected anything, we would blame a kid named Calvin so that everyone in the school would go looking for *him* instead of the real criminals.'

'Clever,' I whispered.

'That's where you messed up,' Gavin said. 'You told us Eli had something to do with it on Monday.'

'You *what?*' Adam shouted. '*You didn't tell them it was Calvin?*'

Sophia's eyes grew fierce. 'I *did*! But *after* I'd already mentioned Eli by accident! I couldn't think straight because Hotcakes was actually missing! This whole week has been a disaster for me, and you know what? I regret the entire thing!' She looked back at Principal Davis andsaid, 'None of this was worth the trouble,

and I shouldn't have gone along with it.
Hotcakes could be anywhere by now and it's all
my fault for playing along with this dumb idea.'

I stepped forward with a smug look on my
face. 'I think you'll be happy to hear that
Hotcakes is back in his cage backstage,' I said.

Sophia let out a long gasp as her eyes
widened. '*Really? He's back in his cage and safe?*'

I nodded. 'Yup,' I said, and then I started
telling her about how I was the one who found
her penguin, but the principal interrupted me.

'We can sort all this out when your parents get here,' Principal Davis said, gesturing for the three guilty students to walk to his office. 'For now, I'm just glad this is over.'

Sophia punched Adam's arm as they walked away. 'You better be glad Hotcakes is alright! I love that stinkin' bird with all my heart and if anything happened to him, it'd be the *end* of you.'

Principal Davis glanced at Coach Cooper. Both of them shook their heads at each other as they escorted the students back to the office.

Gavin and I watched everyone walk away. He turned back to me and laughed victoriously. I couldn't help but laugh too.

'Wow,' Gavin said. 'I can't believe they all just gave each other up like that!'

'To be fair,' I said, 'Adam *tried* to keep the lie going.'

Wiping his hands together, Gavin acted as if he were dusting them off. 'After a week like this, I think the two of us deserve some ice cold soft drinks.'

I chuckled. 'Make mine orange and you got a deal.'

The crowd in the cafeteria exploded with applause and cheers. I panicked, my throat tightening at the sound. Probably because my whole week had been a nonstop roller-coaster of terrible-ness, and I wasn't sure how much more I could handle.

In my head, I went through the list of what achievements we had unlocked – the kid in the hockey mask had been caught, everyone in the talent show was saved from getting drenched in paint, the talent show itself was still on, the kids behind the evil scheme had been caught, Hotcakes had been returned *safely* to his cage, my ninja clan was going to have a new place to train, *and* a mysterious white ninja appeared who was on my side!

I breathed a sigh of relief at the thought of all the good we had accomplished. So whatever was happening in the cafeteria at that moment couldn't have been bad, right?

The door cracked open an inch, and Faith

poked her head out. 'You guys gotta see this,' she said, upset.

Gavin and I went back into the cafeteria. The crowd continued cheering as we slowly made our way around the cafeteria until we could see the stage.

Onstage was with Hotcakes' cage with him safely inside. Standing next to the cage was Wyatt, waving to the crowd. And next to Wyatt, stood Sebastian, holding a microphone in his hand and smiling like a hero.

'This is such a glorious day!' Sebastian said into the microphone, his voice booming from the speakers. 'Buchanan's very own hall monitor captain has found the missing penguin and returned it to safety!'

The sixth graders applauded again. Strange how quickly they were able to forget all the terrible things Wyatt had done. I almost envied their forgetfulness.

'I want everyone in here to know that good deeds do *not* go unnoticed, and that bad kids *can* become good!' Sebastian continued.

'What's he gonna...' Faith whispered, trailing off.

'And that's why I'd like to announce that I'm promoting Wyatt to *Vice President of Buchanan School*!' Sebastian said joyfully.

Everyone in the room cheered. Students were so excited about Hotcakes being rescued that a few of them even fainted.

'What!' Zoe shouted, but she was drowned out by all the shouting. 'Can he do that?'

Gavin folded his arms. 'Sebastian does whatever he wants in this school. Principal Davis doesn't seem to care if it doesn't cause any trouble.'

'Um, Wyatt being the vice president sounds like trouble to me!' Zoe said.

Faith shot a look of disbelief at me. 'Is this really happening?'

I didn't know what to say so I shrugged. It was still early in the morning, and I had already gone through *so much* that it really *did* feel like a dream.

Sebastian tapped on the microphone, and said, 'So let's all celebrate with an amazing talent show put on by one of Buchanan's most prized students – Zoe!'

The spotlight swung around the room and landed on Zoe. She stood to attention and blinked. She glanced back at me

'The show must go on, right?' I said. 'I'll be fine.'

Zoe's expression shifted to curiosity.

'A real hero doesn't need to take credit for

every good thing they do,' I said, repeating her wise words.

She flashed me a smile. Her mouth didn't say thank you, but her eyes did. After grabbing a microphone from a nearby stand, she jogged to the front of the cafeteria.

Gavin and Faith sat on the metal chairs next to the sounding-board.

I leaned against the back wall of the cafeteria, watching Wyatt step off the stage. Carlyle and a bunch of red ninjas in their street clothes met him at the steps, congratulating him.

Part of me felt sad that I wasn't going to get so much as a nod of approval from anyone for saving the day, but that feeling passed quickly when I remembered Zoe's words.

Being a ninja isn't about fame and popularity; it's about honour, loyalty and family. Once I realised that, the sad feeling I had sorta just... vanished.

Letting my eyes drift across the room, I saw Zoe on the stage cracking jokes and making kids laugh as she started the show. She was a natural performer, that was for sure. Everyone in the room was there simply because she wanted to throw an amazing party in the form of a talent show. She wasn't doing this for herself; she was doing it for the students of Buchanan.

Wyatt was off to the side of the cafeteria. And I suddenly realised something else...

I *wasn't* angry.

Sure, this had been an awful week for me with an almost nonstop shower of terror soaking me to my bones, but as I watched Zoe on the stage, all those angry feelings disappeared. Zoe was smiling – *really smiling* – and that was when I realised that I didn't care if Wyatt got credit for finding Hotcakes.

So what? It's more important that Hotcakes was safe and unhurt. I'm just happy that Sophia can rest easy knowing her pet that she *loves* is safe.

President Sebastian promoting Wyatt to vice president was another thing. It was *so* obvious that something was going on there, and that

their part of the story was *far* from over, but
standing in the cafeteria at that moment,
I chuckled and shook my head. Whatever was
happening could wait until next week. If I just
stewed on my anger, then I'd miss out on the
things that mattered and made me happy. And
for me, it was seeing my cousin happily talking
on stage to the whole sixth grade.

I smiled again. Coincidently, Faith looked over and smiled at me right at that second. I'm glad the room was dark because I'm pretty sure I blushed.

I had a goofy grin on my face, but Hotcakes was safe, Zoe was happy, and the talent show could go on exactly as planned. My cousin was about to put on a killer show, and I was able to watch it. Life was alright. No…life was *good*.

And to me, that was worth way more than a thousand bucks.

Diary of a 6th Grade Ninja series

Collect
the
SET!

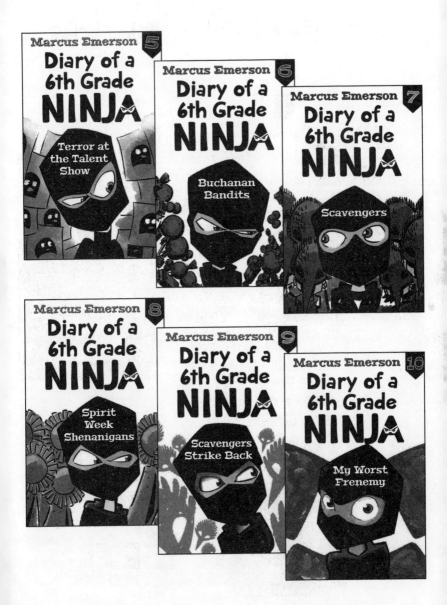

Marcus Emerson is the author of several highly imaginative children's books, including the 6th Grade Ninja series, the Secret Agent 6th Grader series, *Lunchroom Wars* and the Adventure Club series. His goal is to create children's books that are engaging, funny, and inspirational for kids of all ages – even the adults who secretly never grew up.

Marcus Emerson is currently having the time of his life with his beautiful wife and their amazing children. He still dreams of becoming an astronaut someday and walking on Mars.